For Andrew, Allyson, and Aidan—keep dreaming,
stay curious, and be grateful. Your lives are gifts, and
I'm proud to be part of them.

CONTENTS

INTRODUCTION

In my youth, I would watch reruns of the original *Twilight Zone*. It was one of my favorite television shows. The opening music and visuals filled me with a sense of anticipatory excitement. I had a short attention span, and the episodes were just the right length. They caught my imagination like few other shows could. They had great variety—science fiction, alternate history, magical realism—and often finished with a twist. They exposed and magnified the good and evil of human nature. Some of the stories were dark cautionary tales, others were lighthearted and even humorous.

The ten stories in this collection are my attempt to capture that feeling of my youth. At least half of the stories are science fiction; the rest might be better classified as speculative fiction or even magical realism. In any case, they are intended to follow the spirit of those original *Twilight Zone* episodes. I tried to replicate that variety of genres, themes, and plot twists that I believe helped make *The Twilight Zone* so unique and fascinating.

I've included a brief introduction to each tale. I'm often asked where my stories come from, and I wish I had a simple answer for that. A few of my darker tales came from dreams. Unfortunately, I rarely remember my dreams, so many are scratched out of everyday events, thoughts, fears, and memories. A few of the stories just flowed out of me, like magic. Others were laborious efforts, fighting me along the way. But whatever their journeys, these stories are the ones that made it to the end—the evolutionary survivors. Other ideas were discarded, some before the first word was written; others, fully formed, were cut based on the good advice of friends and editors. I hope you enjoy reading them as much as I enjoyed writing them.

So, join me on a journey to a new dimension. A place that lies between my imagination and fears. A destination that is as vast as the universe and as old as time. A place you only find between light and darkness. Welcome to: *Ten Tales of a Dark Tomorrow.*

As I've been lucky enough to witness firsthand, there is little in this world as powerful as the love of a mother for her daughter. On a somewhat unrelated note, I've long been fascinated with the concept of parallel worlds. This tale is the intersection of those two tidbits, and it tests the limits of a mother's love.

My Little Girl

I watch the snow fall silently outside my window. It seems to only deepen my dread. It's warm inside, but I shiver anyway. Thankfully, she's sleeping in this morning. Even though I just woke up, I'm tired. Not sleepy, but tired of worrying, tired of wondering when it's going to happen next. I'm tired of trying to understand it all. And despite everything, I miss him—mainly because I feel so alone.

"Morning, Mama."

She climbs into the chair with me, nearly spilling my coffee. I pull the afghan around her, and she snuggles in. She's so little, so light, that I barely feel the weight of her. But I feel the warmth of her.

"Morning, sweetie."

She says nothing, content to burrow into my chest. I look at the top of her head: thick blond hair, a line of pink scalp at her part. She's wicked smart for her age, and I'm still trying to get used to that. The doctors have used words like *gifted*, *genius*, and *prodigy*. She plays piano pieces that most couldn't master at any age. She can multiply three-digit numbers in her head instantly. She reads voraciously and beat me in chess the first time we played. People say she is a gift. I smile, but only I know what she is. She's my child, but she isn't—she's a version, a duplicate.

The snow starts falling more heavily, in big, thick flakes. It looks so quiet and peaceful outside.

"Are you hungry, honey?"

She stays quiet, and I won't push. I never push. But still, it's so important to keep her from being hungry and overtired. Anything to avoid the tantrums.

I sip my coffee. It's cooled off a bit, and I want to reheat it in the microwave, but I won't. I won't disturb her silence.

I glance at yesterday's paper on the end table. I haven't even opened it yet for fear of what I'll read. Already, I've discovered that North Korea has developed nuclear weapons, Donald Trump is president, and Disney owns Star Wars. All facts that everyone seems to take for granted but that shake me to my core. Not in and of themselves—I couldn't care less who owns Star Wars. But because they aren't part of my reality. At least, they weren't a few months ago.

"Pancakes," she finally says.

I love her, but I don't. She's my daughter, but she isn't. She's little and fragile, and she needs me, but she frightens me. She's three years old. She's just three years old.

"OK. Let me up, honey."

She gives me a sweet little hug and then crawls out of the chair. I grab my coffee and head to the kitchen. I find the griddle, plug it in, and take a moment to heat up my coffee. I hear the piano from the living room. It's a haunting, melancholy piece I've never heard before. She's probably composing it on the fly. As I gather the pancake mix, an egg, and the mixing bowl, I think about the first time it happened.

Seven months earlier

"Maybe she shouldn't go on any more rides," I said. "I don't want her to get sick."

It was eight thirty on a Saturday night, and it was a perfect summer evening. But my senses get overwhelmed easily, and even though this was just a little pop-up carnival in the mall parking lot, I was feeling frazzled. It seemed like every person in town had decided to come out.

"What do you mean?" Mason asked. "She's having a blast! It's not like she's going on the Tilt-A-Whirl or anything. Besides, I bought ten dollars' worth of tickets. We might as well use them up."

The crowd was enough on its own, but the combination of smells, sounds, and lights was making my head swim and my stomach rumble. The corn dog I'd eaten threatened to make a reappearance.

"Honestly, I guess it's me who's feeling sick. I don't think that corn dog is agreeing with me."

I've always had the tendency to project myself onto her. If I'm cold, I bundle her up. If I'm hungry, I make her eat.

I was trying to navigate the dense crowd with Candy's little umbrella stroller while Mason walked ahead of me, carrying our daughter through the swarm of people. She had her little blue dress on, the one that reminded me of Dorothy in *The Wizard of Oz*.

Mason stopped and turned back to me. "I didn't know. I'm sorry you're not feeling well, honey." He looked up the midway and then investigated my eyes, trying to gauge my discomfort. "OK, how about we all three go on the merry-go-round? It's three tickets each, so we'll just throw the last one away. One more ride, and then we'll get you home for a Tums and a hot bath."

I looked at Candy in his arms. She was wide-eyed and all smiles. Her lips were still blue from her first snow cone. "That sounds fine. Thanks."

We fought through the crowd and made our way to the merry-go-round. The line was long but not crazy. I put Candy on my shoulders, and Mason passed the time by playing peeka-boo with her.

She kept pointing, and when he asked her what she was looking at, she said "Unicorn" as clear as day. I hadn't known she knew what a unicorn was. But sure enough, the merry-go-round had horses, camels, a lion, an elephant, a rooster, and exactly one unicorn. When it was finally our turn, though, some older girl had already mounted it.

"Unicorn!"

"Candy, someone else is riding the unicorn," I said. "You can ride the lion or one of the horses. You love horses. Look at this beautiful pony."

"Unicorn!"

Mason knelt to her level. "Honey, someone else is on the unicorn. You need to pick another animal."

And with that, Candy lost it. She began to cry—well, more like screech. Mason picked her up, and she kicked and flailed. The little girl on the unicorn just held on tighter, hunch-ing over to hug her prized steed. Mason and I were embarrassed, and with a shared look, we jointly decided to cut our losses and exit the merry-go-round. We walked out the exit and found a little open space off to the side.

Once Candy realized she had lost not just the unicorn but the merry-go-round ride altogether, she dialed it up a notch. She thrashed in Mason's arms so hard that she caught him in the nose with her forehead. It stunned him a bit, and he set her down. That's when it happened.

I noticed a shimmer around Candy. It was sort of a wavy mist that distorted the air around her. For a moment, I thought my corn dog was getting the better of me, but then I saw the look on Mason's face. He was seeing it too. And then, without any further warning, Candy began to fade.

I was five or six steps away from her, so I yelled Mason's name as I sprinted toward her. His hands shot out, but then he paused. I saw fear on his face as his hands hovered just inches away from her.

"For God's sake!" I shouted. I rushed at my fading daughter, but my foot got tangled in the umbrella stroller, knocking it over. "Grab her, Mason!"

He wouldn't do it, and she winked out. She was just gone, completely gone.

My stomach fell away. I finally lost my corn dog on the pavement. It splattered violently in front of my feet.

When I looked up again, she was coming back. Just a flicker at first, but then, thank God, she became solid. Her tantrum had changed from angry screeches to scared whimpers.

Without hesitation, I rushed in and gathered her up. Mason stared, still frozen in fear. I hugged her and stroked her hair, telling her everything was all right.

I looked around. The few people who had noticed our scene were turning away, apparently unwilling or unable to accept what they'd just witnessed. Instead, they forced themselves to be satisfied that the little girl was safe in her mother's arms.

But I couldn't be so easily soothed. I remained panicked, and despite my very firm grip on Candy, alarm bells were still ringing in my brain.

Mason finally broke free of his fear and hugged both of us. "You're OK, Candy. You're just fine. We're OK. Oh God, we're all OK," he chanted.

Candy, still sobbing, buried her face into my neck. As my stomach began to settle and my mind began to clear, I stroked her hair and straightened her yellow dress. "You're OK, sweetie. It was just—" I stopped, my fingers still holding the yellow fabric of the dress.

My mind immediately began to talk itself out of the impossible truths it was facing. I told myself maybe I had just gotten dizzy from the bad corn dog and my upset stomach. Maybe she had, in fact, been wearing her yellow dress instead of the blue all along.

We quickly left the fair, and I sat in the back of the car with Candy, holding her hand the whole way home.

As soon we arrived at home, I ran a warm bath for Candy. I wanted to rinse off the grime of the carnival, but more importantly, I wanted to wash away the strangeness of the night. She looked small and pink against the fluffy white suds.

"Mommy, why did you change your hair?"

Her question rocked me not so much from what she asked, but how clearly she asked it. It was only later that what she asked bothered me as well.

"I didn't change my hair sweetie," I said.

Candy tilted her head, but went back to playing in the tub. She found her plastic horse in the suds and made him gallop across the white foam mountains. I took the opportunity to scrub her back with a washcloth, and when I got to her left shoulder, I froze for an instant. I looked over at the perfect skin on her other shoulder, then I ran my finger across the raised mole on her left. I remembered the doctor's voice from her checkup only three or four days before—*"You're going to want to keep an eye on this mole on her right shoulder. It's most likely nothing, but if it grows larger or takes an irregular shape, let us know right away."*

His voice was crystal clear in my mind, and I would have bet a million dollars he said *right* shoulder. Besides, being a first-time mom, I'd checked the mole on her right shoulder every night since.

I didn't try to talk to Mason about it until after the bath when she fell asleep on the couch next to us.

"Mason, something happened."

"We're fine. Candy's fine. She just had a bad tantrum, and the weird carnival lights made her look strange. She's fine. Everything's fine."

I wanted to believe that. I could almost let myself believe that. But the way she disappeared, the way she cried when she returned, the dress, the mole . . .

"No. Everything is not fine. Something happened."

He shook his head and wouldn't look me in the eyes. "Nothing happened. We're fine."

I grasped his arms, looking directly into his eyes, my voice quavering. "Her mole. Her mole was on her right shoulder, and now it's on her left."

He looked up at the ceiling, sighing. "No. That's not possible. You're still feeling queasy from the carnival. You're questioning everything. You're just remembering it wrong. It was always on the left shoulder. We just need a good night's sleep. Everything is fine."

"She wore her blue dress tonight. I let her choose between the yellow and the blue, and she chose the blue."

"You're just confused, honey," he said. But his eyes were large, and I could see a large vein standing out on his neck. He was trying to convince himself as much as me.

Something occurred to me then. I stood for a moment, then left the room and went straight to Candy's closet. I gasped when I saw the yellow dress hanging there, even though it was exactly what I'd expected—and dreaded. I frantically dug through the rows of colorful outfits for the one thing that could possibly give me comfort, but it was gone. Her Dorothy dress was gone.

I returned to the living room with two identical yellow dresses: the one on its hanger, neat and fresh, and the other, dug out of the hamper, crumpled and still stained with a little of my vomit.

"The blue dress is gone," I announced to Mason, my voice shaking. "But now we have two yellow dresses. And look—they both have a little tear under the left arm." I thrust the dresses out for him to see. "It's the exact same tear on both dresses."

Mason stared at the dresses, swallowed hard, and then turned to me. "What are you saying?"

"It's the same dress, except . . . it's not." I closed my eyes and shook my head. "And she's Candy, except she's not. I don't understand what the hell happened, but she isn't the same. Her mole is different. *She* is different. I know it. A mother just knows. She's very close to our Candy, but she's not her."

That's when I broke down. And even though Mason held me and wiped my tears away, it was the beginning of the end for us. I couldn't forgive him for not grabbing Candy. And he wouldn't accept that something unnatural had happened that night. He wouldn't accept that this Candice wasn't our child.

Some days, I'd try to tell myself he was right. Some days, I'd say I was going insane. But then I'd get out the two yellow dresses and look at the little tear, and deep down, I'd know. I'd picture my little girl with another version of me, though, and that would make it slightly less terrifying.

"Honey, what do you think about counseling?" Mason asked me, coming into the family room and cautiously sitting down on the armchair next to the sofa where I lay. I'd been spending a great deal of time on the sofa. "I mean, it's been two weeks now. We could get some couples counseling, or you could see someone . . .?"

"'Cause you think I'm crazy?" I asked. I spun my finger around my temple.

"No, it's just that—"

I shook my head side to side. "Just stop. Why don't you admit it—you think I'm insane. And maybe I am. But I won't sit on a shrink's couch and try to explain to some stranger how my daughter is not my daughter. I won't tell anyone how she faded away and a different little girl faded back in."

"You don't have to talk about that." He tilted his head, trying to look sympathetic. "It's just . . . you've been so moody. I just want things to go back to normal. You need to get past this."

I stood up. I could feel my face flush. "Back to normal?" I repeated. "Things *aren't* normal! You want me to get past losing my *daughter*? I lost my baby, and I can't even tell anyone about it!"

He gave me a slight, patient smile. It infuriated me. "She's right in the next room, honey. You didn't lose her." He sighed. "OK, so maybe her dress changed. I can admit that something strange happened. But we're OK. And you need to move on with your life."

He was just so *patronizing*. My frustration bubbled over. "*Go to hell, Mason!*" I shouted. "You might be able to forget your daughter, but I can't." I felt hot tears run down my cheeks. "You let her go. You were too afraid to grab her. You were right next to her, and you just let her go!"

I could tell he was fighting off his anger, trying not to escalate. His cheeks reddened and he pursed his lips like he always did when he was pissed off. But right now, I wanted him to yell at me. I knew it wasn't really his fault, but I had to blame someone. It was a cheap way out, but it was the only way I could cope.

Just then, I saw his face change and his eyes dart behind me. I turned and saw Candice. I don't know how long she'd been standing there.

"Park," she said. I wondered if she was trying to distract us from our argument.

"Not now, Candy," he told her. "Mommy and I are discussing something important. Go play in your room for a little bit."

Candice closed her eyes tight and then opened them as she spoke. "I want to swing!"

Since the scene at the carnival happened, I'd relived it over and over again in my head. I was confident that the tantrums had brought on Candy's incident. "Mason, let's just take her to the park," I said, almost pleading.

Mason turned his attention to me. "Honey, we've been spoiling her. We can't keep letting her get her way with everything." He walked over to Candice and knelt in front of her. "Candy, we'll go to the park later. But right now, Mommy and I are talking about something important. You need to go to your room and read your books for a while."

Candy stomped her feet and balled her fists. "No. Park!"

I started to speak, but Mason shot me a glare. He was still livid from my accusations.

"No, Candy. You need to go to your room. Right now!" Mason stood back up and crossed his arms, now glaring at Candice.

Over the last two weeks, I'd been treating her like a china doll. She wasn't used to being yelled at. I saw tears in her eyes, but she seemed to gather herself and turn her fear into anger.

"I wanna swing at the park!" she shouted.

It came on fast after that, pretty much the same as at the carnival. First the shimmer, then the mist began to swirl. Mason took a step backward.

I didn't hesitate. I was still grieving for my Candy, but that didn't mean I didn't love this little girl. I lunged across the room and grabbed her, hoping my touch would stop her from fading.

Instead, the whole room faded away. For a moment, everything was black. I could still feel Candice in my arms, but I couldn't see anything.

Then the room slowly faded back in. Mason was gone, along with the car magazines he'd left on the coffee table. Candice was crying and whimpering again.

I pulled the hair away from her face and stroked her cheek. "It's OK, honey. I'm right here. I'm with you."

So here I am, pouring the pancakes onto the griddle for Candice's breakfast while the snow falls outside. She's still playing the piano. The music ebbs and flows. But somehow, it keeps its structure. I watch a tear fall onto one of the pancakes.

Apparently, in this reality, Mason has already left me, so it's just me and Candice most of the time. Even though most things are the same, there are enough differences that make me feel lost and alone. Just when I start to get my feet under me, I hear a bit of news that reminds me I'm somewhere different, somewhere else. In this somewhere, Prince and Tom Petty are dead, and the world seems a little darker because of it.

But every day, I fall a little more in love with Candice—with this new Candy. Yes, she's different. But she's still sweet and loving, and I've already decided that if she goes again, I'm going with her. Of course, I'd rather avoid another tantrum, because I'm scared of what's in the next world, the next version of reality. But if she goes, so do I. I can't bear to lose my daughter again.

At least we'll have each other. And whatever tomorrow brings, we'll face it together.

The End

This is one of the tales that came to me in a dream. I woke up in the middle of the night with a jumbled story not too far from the one below bouncing around in my head. I got out of bed and jotted down the gist. When I sat down to write it in the light of day, it flowed out so easily that I feared it was a movie or a short story I had read long ago. However, I've done quite a bit of searching, and while there are plenty of similar plotlines and tropes (haven't they all been written at this point?), it appears my subconscious didn't downright plagiarize. I was surprised to find myself enjoying writing a bit of horror; my id seems to have a dark side.

TERROR ON PANDOR-3

It's a plum job, really, my little taxi service. Coming out of the academy, I couldn't have dreamed of better. The key was to be dead center in the middle. You see, the top pilots were scooped up by the military or other branches of the government.

Some might fly for elite families. I guess that might not be so bad. But you don't want to get in the middle of family politics. Overhear the wrong thing on a long trip, and you'll end up losing your job. Or, more likely, turn up dead from a "freak" accident. Yeah, best not to get involved with the families.

"Pandor-2 Mission Control, this is *Texas Five*," I say into the headset. "Comm check."

On the other hand, you don't want to be at the bottom of your academy class. You end up flying interstellar freighters at the ass end of the galaxy, maybe hauling ore from some desolate mining operation to a processing center on a dead world. Back and forth until retirement or until you die from a microasteroid hit, whichever comes first.

No, trust me—it's best to be in the middle. And luckily, I had the street smarts to figure that out early. Yep, the best jobs are in the middle—gigs like hauling business executives for small companies or transporting rare goods for an import-export company. Short hops and good pay.

"This is Mission Control," a voice replies. It's Sam. "Reading you loud and clear, *Texas Five*."

But even with my street smarts, I must admit, I got lucky. I'm the pilot for a small long-term archaeological project in the Pandor system. I haul supplies and occasionally transport the people on Pandor-3's five-person archaeological team. The lucky part is that Pandor-3 is about a two-day hop from Pandor-2, which is also known as Planet Paradise.

"Thanks, Sam," I say. "Flight plan is filed. Preflight check is complete."

Planet Paradise is about as perfect as you can get: just the right distance from its sun, an incredibly stable climate, nothing alive that wants to eat you, and as far as we can tell, the best beaches in the galaxy. Sure, you might get a little rainstorm in the afternoon, but it clouds up, drops some gentle rain, and then clears up again in about forty-five minutes. The bars and casinos are lively, and the golf courses are amazing.

"You're number seven in line, Charlie. Good to fuel."

So over the last two years, I've ended up splitting my time between Pandor-3 and Paradise. And it just so happens that I've ended up with a decent amount of free time on Paradise. Needless to say, my golf game is fantastic, and my tan isn't bad either. The Pandor system is practically smack-dab in the middle of everything important. It's "on the way" to just about any destination of the rich and famous. So, while my luck in the casinos is only average, my luck with the ladies has been, shall we say, stellar.

"Fuel tanks open," I say. "Number seven? Can't you push me up on the list a bit?"

"Just doing my job," Sam says back with a chuckle.

Just imagine a steady stream of rich, beautiful women. They've been cooped up on a passenger ship for two or three months—tight quarters, zero G, freeze-dried food, you get the idea. And then they disembark on Paradise, with its perfect weather, beaches, gourmet food, and the best drinks anywhere. Case in point: they make better tequila on Pandor-2 than on Earth. Anyway, they step off, get a massage, do a quick workout, relax on the beach, and have a Pandor margarita. And who happens to be on the chaise lounge next to them? 'Tis I, a blond, tan, fit, academy-trained space pilot, a bona fide rocketman.

I've tried to stay away from the married ones, which isn't too hard since marriages get rarer every year anyway. Of course, I'd be lying if I said it never happened. They don't always wear their rings on Paradise.

So yeah. This job has been a pretty good gig.

"You're at number four now, Charlie. Fuel umbilicals open. Where you headed?"

"Same old, same old," I say. "Resupply to Pandor-3, no passengers. Fuel tanks to one hundred percent."

Unlike Planet Paradise, Pandor-3 is awful. It's a cold, empty gray planet like so many others. But apparently, there are some ancient alien remains buried there. The good news is that the research facility is above average. They have individual sleeping compartments and a full entertainment system. Still, it's not a place you'd want to spend the holidays.

Here's the thing, though: I can't wait to get there.

"Umbilicals separated," Sam says. "I hear the weather's real nice on Pandor-3: sunny, clear skies, and about minus one hundred fifty degrees Celsius at night. You're number two now."

"Funny, Sam. Not there for the weather. Craft is ready for launch. I've got all greens here."

You see, I think I'm falling in love. Yeah, I know—why the hell would I go and do that? Trust me, didn't plan it and didn't want it. But apparently, I don't get to choose. She's not even my type. Athletic build instead of my usual, uh, let's say, *curvaceous* gals. She's incredibly smart, opinionated, and independent—three traits I typically try to avoid. It's a lot easier to jump on a shuttle and fly away from a girl you can barely talk to. I also normally go for blonde and blue eyed, but Camille has curly dark hair, gorgeous brown eyes, and the most perfect brown skin you have ever seen.

She doesn't know it yet. I've been trying to play it cool. Well, she may suspect. It's not easy to hide how I feel. This last stay on Paradise, she was all I thought about. My golf game fell apart, and I passed on every woman who made a pass at me. After eighteen days in Paradise, all I want is to launch outta here and get back to a desolate, lifeless planet.

Oh, and to top it off, she's married.

"Okay, *Texas Five*," Sam begins. "You are number one on the pad. Range is go for launch; control is go for launch. You may launch when ready."

She's not married to a human. At least there's that. No, she's married to her job. She's the chief archaeologist on the Pandor-3 dig. Apparently, she's one of the top experts in the galaxy on the ancients. I looked her up. She was top of her class at university. Wrote some groundbreaking papers. Passed up a prestigious government position on Earth and took a field job instead. And unfortunately, she's hopelessly dedicated to the dig.

"Control," I say, "I'm starting final countdown. Three . . . two . . . one . . . launch. I have good ignition."

Still, I'm going to tell her during this resupply, and this calm, steely-eyed rocket jockey is nervous as hell. Every time I think about telling her, I start sweating and my heart starts racing. It's because I already know her answer, but I don't care. I can hear her now. *It would interfere with my work.* Maybe she would sleep with me once or twice, but that's not what I want. I want to marry her. Jesus, what am I saying? I'm a mess.

"*Texas Five*, we have good telemetry. Launch looks good from here. Safe journey, Charlie."

I have two days to think about it. Two days to wrestle over every word of my pitch. Two days until I see those mesmerizing dark eyes and her flawless skin. Oh God, I'm in deep. What the hell is wrong with me?

"Roger that, Sam. I'm nearing orbit. One loop around Paradise, and I'll be off. See you in two and a half weeks."

"Maurice, are you going to help me unload or what?"

I'm standing in the rear air lock, calling loudly. Not that I'm expecting any fanfare for my arrival, but someone usually at least acknowledges me. All I get is silence.

"Maurice? Camille? Anyone? Anyone home?"

It's unsettling. They're usually a loud, talkative bunch. And Kat likes her music. I don't think I've ever heard the facility silent like this.

I enter the main living area. The large glass window on the far wall shows the rocky, dusty gray landscape outside. To the left is a lush green forest.

As I step toward the window, a sudden movement startles me. But it's just a young doe in the forest darting from view. It's Camille's favorite screen saver on the wall viewer. The forest scene looks more real than the window, which is the idea, I guess.

I pass through the living room and toward the hallway. It leads to sleeping quarters, a gym, and bathrooms on the right and labs on the left. At the end of the hall sit the control room and the kitchen. Just as I enter the hallway, I hear a thump from the far end.

"Charlie, is that you? I'm over here."

I continue down the hall to the control room, where Maurice is huddled over the main console. He has a headset on. The control room provides a variety of readouts of anyone performing an EVA at the dig or in the nearby area. Based on the monitor, it looks like all four of the other crew members are out on an EVA.

"It's so quiet in here I thought I was walking into a surprise party or something," I say.

Maurice finally turns and gives me a large smile. He shakes my hand, and I try not to wince. Although short, he's incredibly strong and muscle bound.

"Welcome back, Charlie. I'm sorry. Big commotion out there. They found something, and they've done nothing but argue all morning."

Maurice is the cook. Well, more than the cook. He's the nutritional technician, facility maintenance engineer, physical trainer, and backup medical specialist. But I mostly think of him as the cook, because he's a darn good one. Maurice is my best friend on the crew. Unlike the rest of them, Maurice and I have one thing very much in common: neither of us wants anything to do with archaeology.

"What did they find?"

"They don't know, or they won't tell me. They're very concerned about mission guidelines, agency protocols, and archaeometry policy or something like that. Well, yesterday they found a box or a vault or a tomb. They can't even agree on what to call it. They found it about five kilometers to the west."

"What were they doing so far west?"

"Apparently, Kat did a geophysical signal survey on a hunch. Took the equipment out without permission. Said she had a 'feeling.'" He places his hands on his heart at the word *feeling*.

"That must have driven Winston crazy," I say.

"He's been going crazy the whole time. Wants to shut down the entire operation. Hence all the arguments about guidelines and protocols. Camille keeps overruling him. He's about to go ballistic. I've never seen them argue like this. And today, in spite of his objections, they all went out to open the vault."

I turn and look at the monitors. Maurice is right: it looks like they're still fighting. Winston's heart rate and blood pressure are both in the yellow. I find that somewhat amusing, but mostly, I'm frustrated that this vault thing will be competing for Camille's attention.

"Did they get it open?"

Maurice shrugs. "I think so. Like I said, all I hear is a bunch of archaeological mumbo jumbo. But I think they opened it, and now they're arguing about bringing something into the labs."

He flips a switch on the console. "Folks. Hey, team." The only response to Maurice's call is muffled bickering. He rolls his eyes at me, then turns back to the screen. "*Hey, team!*" he says with some force. "Charlie's here. He and I are going to unload the *Texas Five*. Whatever you decide, you can reach us on the facility intercom."

"Hi, Charlie," Camille says with a little wave. My heart skips just seeing her smile. "We've actually already decided, Maurice."

"*You* decided," Winston says.

Camille ignores Winston and continues. "We're bringing it in. We'll ping you when we get to the front door."

Maurice leans in and turns off the comm. He takes off his headset and sets it on the console.

"I'm not listening to that shit anymore today. Let's go unload your boat."

"We're at the front door," Camille says over the intercom, her voice peppered with a little static. "We might need a little help out here."

"I'll go," Maurice tells me. "You hold things down in here."

Maurice is being a good friend. He knows I'm not a fan of space suits. Sure, I made it through all the training. I successfully completed an external inspection a month ago on the crew's emergency evacuation ship. But I just don't like them. It's everything: the breathing, the restrictive movement, the knowing you're a seam pop away from death. Let me put it this way: I prefer to fly through the void of space rather than walk through it.

I depress the intercom button. "Maurice is getting suited up now," I say. I follow Maurice to the front air lock to help him suit up. Once I help him out of the facility, I go back into the control room to watch. A large perfectly spherical shiny glass globe sits in the back of the big rover. It seems impossible the object could have been unearthed from this dusty gray planet.

Camille and Kat are edging it toward the back of the rover bed, where Maurice and Winston wait. The glass ball must be over three feet in diameter, which means it will be a tight fit in the air-lock hatch. Maurice lifts it off the rover while Winston unsuccessfully tries to help. Winston is tall and gangly, all arms and legs. His head is so big, I'm surprised it fits in his helmet.

"We're coming in three and two," Camille says. "Kat and Vicky will be right behind us."

I hustle to the air lock that they call the front door. The *Texas Five* is attached to the other air lock, the back door. I see Maurice, Winston, and Camille inside. Camille gives me the thumbs-up, and I open the inner door. I help Winston and Camille get out of their suits. Camille and I remove only Maurice's helmet and leave his suit. He doesn't want to put the thing down. Damn, he's strong.

"Let's get it into the main lab," Camille orders. "Put it in the big sink. We'll give it a chemical bath for decontamination. Go—now."

Camille points the way, and Maurice trudges through the facility, tracking dust through the main living area. Camille is normally a clean freak, but this time, she obviously doesn't care.

"Decontamination?" Winston says. "Camille, you've already contaminated the entire facility. Do you know how many protocols you're breaking? And we'll need to send a communication to the Central Archaeology Agency."

"That's enough, Winston. The entire facility is built to be decontaminated. That's why it has the heavy-duty air filtration system. We bring artifacts in all the time. As for contacting the CAA, if we send a communication about this, they'll shut us down for a year while all the various parties fight over next steps and ownership. We have all the proper permissions to dig on this planet and to withdraw and examine artifacts."

"But this is different," he presses. "This might be advanced technology or highly preserved alien biomaterial. Either of those is governed by completely different regulations. There are communication requirements. In those cases—"

"*Stop*," Camille says. "The key word is *might*. We don't know. First, we need to determine what it is. Besides, I have the latitude to improvise in unusual situations. That's what I'm doing: improvising."

Winston starts to protest again, but Camille cuts him off.

"I know you're just doing your job. Your objections will be noted and recorded. But this is my decision, and you won't be held responsible. Now, stop arguing before I have Kat throw you out the air lock."

Camille and Winston disappear down the hallway after Maurice. I stay behind to assist Kat and Vicky as they enter through the air lock. I help Kat first. She's an archaeologist first and technologist second, and she's basically number two in this operation. She worships Camille. Sometimes I catch Kat looking at Camille and wonder if I'm not the only one with romantic interests. But like I said, Camille is married to her job.

Kat finally wrestles free of her suit. "Do you think they've already started the laser ultrasound?"

"I doubt it. You're hardly two minutes behind them. Winston is probably still protesting."

"I'm going to kill that little shit," Kat mutters.

She takes off down the hall, leaving me with Vicky. Vicky is the primary medical specialist at the facility. She's also an expert on ancient alien anatomy. One night, she made a pass at me, and I refused her. She's a beautiful woman, but I had already fallen for Camille. We've had a tenuous relationship ever since. She gives me an icy stare as I help her with her suit.

I try a question to break the silence. "What's inside this crazy glass globe that's got everyone so worked up?"

She sighs, apparently irritated with my attempt at small talk. "Hard to tell. It's full of an opaque silvery liquid. Looks sort of like mercury. But there's definitely something else inside. Sometimes, when you move it, you can see it bounce up against the side. We have a guess, but you'll think we're crazy."

"Try me."

"It's pallium. I'd bet my medical license on it."

"Pallium?"

Vicky rolls her eyes. "The folds and bulges on a cerebral cortex. Charlie, it looks like an enormous humanoid brain."

I raise an eyebrow at her as I finish freeing her from the suit. "You *are* crazy."

"I know. That's why everyone is going batshit. They did an on-site carbon dating of the vault, and it matched the rest of the site—a hundred thousand years old. No way an alien organ that old could be preserved so well. Come on, let's go see what they've got."

As I try to wrap my head around the impossibility of a perfectly preserved hundred-thousand-year-old alien brain, Vicky and I make our way to the main lab. It's made for two people to work comfortably, but all four of the others have somehow squeezed in. Maurice attempts to move the globe from the sink to the laser ultrasound, but once again, Winston is in the way. Eventually, they manage to shuffle around so Maurice can set down the globe.

"This will take a few minutes," Camille says, in full command mode. "Maurice, go get your suit off. Vicky, get in here—we'll need your opinion on this ultrasound. Winston, get out of Vicky's way."

I follow Maurice back to the air lock to help him with his suit.

"Damn, that globe is awkward. Not to mention heavy. I swear Winston almost made me drop it twice." He's scratching vigorously above his ear.

I clear my throat. "Vicky said there might be a preserved alien brain inside."

He shakes his head. He looks exhausted just thinking about it. "The whole galaxy will go mad when they get word of this. Camille is smart to hold off. This place will get locked down, and we'll all be out on our asses."

"Shit. I hadn't thought of that."

I don't want to lose the gig. But even more than that, I don't want to lose Camille.

I finally get Maurice out of his suit. As we exit the air lock, the rest of the group returns to the living room.

"Everyone take a seat," says Camille. "Now that the globe is decontaminated and we've done a quick ultrasound, let's discuss this as a group. I know emotions are high right now, but I'd appreciate it if everyone could take a deep breath and help me think about this logically."

"About time," Winston declares, collapsing onto the nearest seat in a huff.

The rest of us sit down on the couches placed in a U around the wall viewer, which still displays the forest. I sit directly across from Camille and try to meet her gaze, but she's busy ignoring Winston. I look out the real window and notice a small whirlwind whip up the gray dust and then vanish.

"Vicky, what's your opinion on the ultrasound?" Camille begins. "What did you see?"

"Oh, it's definitely a brain. No doubt. It's very similar to a human brain, except for its size, obviously. Two hemispheres, a complex layered structure. There's clearly a pallium, cerebellum, thalamus, hypothalamus, and medulla. The hypothalamus is proportionally larger than a human brain's, and there's a large structure between the hypothalamus and the thalamus that I can't identify. It might be a tumor, or it might be a unique brain structure. That is, that's what I noticed in the few minutes I had with it. I'd like to do a more detailed analysis."

"Maybe it is a tumor," Maurice offers, "and they were preserving the brain so future generations could use it to find a cure? Like their version of cryopreservation?"

"Or perhaps it's their form of mummification, like the ancient Egyptians," Kat says, rubbing her temples.

"I appreciate the thinking," says Camille, "but let's leave its purpose or intent for later. Right now, I'd like to focus on two things: First, let's think about additional testing or analyses we can perform. And then, let's step back and think about our next steps from a mission standpoint. Let's take ideas for analyses first."

"Well," replies Kat, "short of breaching the globe, the only nonintrusive equipment we have is the quantum ultrasound. We would need a chip or sample of the brain matter to do anything like carbon dating."

"We can't breach the globe," says Winston. "I've put up with a great deal, but I cannot allow an artifact of this importance to be compromised without communication and proper protocol."

"No one is suggesting we make any attempt to break the globe, Winston," Camille says, followed by a deep exhale. She reaches back and massages her neck.

"I'd like to do a more extensive exam with the quantum ultrasound," says Vicky. "I could do a full-detail mapping and comparison to the human brain."

"Makes sense. Any other ideas, analysis-wise?"

Everyone is quiet as Camille makes eye contact with each person. Her gaze seems to linger longer on me, but maybe it's just wishful thinking on my part.

"Then let's move on to our next steps mission-wise," she says. "I realize—"

"Wait. Hold on. Before we move on to that, has anyone noticed . . ." Kat pauses like she's gathering courage, like she's about to cross some threshold. "An . . . itch in their brain?"

Every head turns toward her.

Kat continues, avoiding eye contact. "I'm probably just imagining it, but every once in a while, I—"

Maurice jumps in. "Yeah, I felt it when I was carrying the blasted thing into the lab. Itch is a good word, but it was almost like something was poking around inside my head."

"Are you suggesting that the globe is responsible?" Winston asks, incredulous. "No. This is just the power of suggestion. Maurice, you're imagining it because Kat planted the idea." He crosses his arms and sits back in his chair, as if daring someone else to speak up.

"No, Winston—I felt it too," says Camille, leaning forward. "It's very subtle. I thought I was imagining it, but if Kat and Maurice felt it . . . How about you, Vicky? Feel anything like that?"

Vicky's head is down, but she nods.

Camille turns to me. I look around at everyone, not sure what to say. Internally, I'm leaning toward Winston's theory about the power of suggestion. But I'm not about to side with Winston. "Look, I haven't felt a thing, but I wasn't out there retrieving it. If you all felt it, I believe you."

"Thanks, Charlie," Camille says, allowing a small smile to cross her lips for just a moment before she turns back to the group. "Everyone, we need to take this seriously. Is there any chance that this brain could be alive?"

"Of course not," Winston says with a nervous laugh.

"We know these aliens were far more advanced than us," Vicky says. "We don't know what's possible right now."

"What if . . . what if it's trying to communicate?" Kat asks.

Camille furrows her brow, carefully thinking the suggestion over. "Vicky, you're our medical specialist," she says. "Do you think that sort of thing is even possible? Could this thing be trying to communicate with us?"

Vicky nods slowly. "It's somewhat outside my field of study, but I would say yes. There are all kinds of technologies being developed for brain-to-brain communication. It's very possible this species could have developed that technology too. The brain might be equipped with it, or it might have evolved with this sort of capability. I would be more skeptical, but . . . I definitely felt it."

"I told you, this is the power of suggestion," Winston says. But I can see fear in his eyes. "You're all crazy. But on the off chance that it *is* true, then it's more important than ever to return it to its vault."

"For the first time ever," Vicky says, with a tremor in her voice, "I have to agree with Winston. If this brain is alive and capable of brain-to-brain communication, we need to isolate it until the proper controls are in place. We need to return it to the vault and call it in."

Suddenly, Kat stands. There's something about her look, but I dismiss it. Everything is so crazy anyway.

"I have to get something from the kitchen," she says, striding out of the room.

"Let's slow down here," says Camille. She leans back in her seat. "I want you all to realize that if we call this in and we hear back, we're done. We'll be shut down, and they'll bring in government people. They'll bring in the military. This dig will be over for years, maybe longer. I think Vicky should at least do her detailed scan first. We should also think about any final surveys at the site. Winston, even you were pretty excited about that sealed chamber in section three."

Kat returns from the kitchen. She has a large grin on her face, like she's about to perform a prank on someone. She walks behind Vicky, yanks her by the hair, and deftly thrusts a large kitchen knife into her neck.

Camille screams. To be honest, I think I do as well.

Paralyzed, I watch as Maurice immediately moves behind Kat and grabs her in a bear hug. Vicky's mouth opens, but I only hear gurgling sounds.

Kat struggles against Maurice while trying to pull the knife from Vicky's neck. It must be lodged firmly in her spine.

With Vicky's blood spurting vigorously, Kat's soaked hand keeps slipping off the knife.

Maurice finally manages to pull Kat away. Camille leaps toward Vicky, grabbing a blanket from the couch and holding it against her neck.

"We have to get the brain into the vault!" Winston screams as he stares at the blood. "Now! We have to get the brain back into the vault!"

Maurice drags Kat back down the hallway. She struggles furiously.

I finally gain control of my legs and go to Camille. "Should—should I try to remove the knife?" I stammer. Vicky is slumped on the couch.

"No. Hold this blanket and apply pressure the best you can. I'll get the medical kit."

We switch places, and she takes off down the hallway. Vicky is looking at me, eyes wide. Her mouth keeps opening and closing, but now there's no sound.

"Hang in there, Vicky. Camille went to get the medical kit."

I should be paying more attention, but I can hear the chaos of Maurice and Kat wrestling in the kitchen. I'm desperate for Camille to return and don't notice the air-lock door opening behind me.

When Camille finally does return with the medical kit, her eyes are focused on something behind me.

"Where are you going, Winston?" she cries. "Wait! We need you here."

I want to look, but I stay focused on Vicky's neck. I only hear the air lock close behind me. Camille fumbles with the medical kit and finally pulls out a couple of items.

"OK, you go stop Winston while I try to stop the bleeding," she orders.

Once again, we switch positions. I think I see Vicky's eyes glaze over, but I do as I'm told. I look in the air lock and see that Winston has just pulled his suit on.

"Winston, stop! Where are you going?"

His eyes are wild as he begins to work the outer-door mechanism.

"Winston, *stop!*" I yell. "You don't even have your helmet on!"

I pound on the air-lock door, but Winston doesn't seem to hear me. The outer door opens. Winston takes one step—and then collapses outside the door. I keep pounding on the door even after I know he's dead.

Camille's sobbing brings me out of it. I press the code to close the outer door, turn, and go to her.

A large medical pad covers Vicky's wound, but blood is already soaking through. The knife is on the couch next to them. The couch is soaked with blood. Camille's head is against Vicky's chest. I put my hand on her shoulder. She's shaking. She turns to me, her face wet and red.

"She's gone."

She falls into me, and I hold her tightly, stroking her back. This is not the way I pictured our first embrace. My stomach is still doing flip-flops from seeing all the blood.

Maurice bursts back into the room. "What the fuck is going on?"

"We don't know. Vicky is dead, and Winston just walked out of the air lock without a goddamned helmet." Camille sobs into my chest, and it occurs to me that she might not have noticed what happened with Winston. I hold her tighter and turn back to Maurice. "Where's Kat?" I ask.

"She's tied up in the kitchen. I used zip ties—double. Fought me like a fucking mountain lion. It took everything I had to restrain her. Jesus, what the hell is happening?"

"It must be the globe," I say. "It controlled them—Kat and Winston both. They had the same crazed look on their faces. It had Kat first, but when you restrained her, it went to Winston. I don't think it liked his suggestion of returning it to the vault." I don't want to believe what I'm saying, but I know it's true.

Camille lifts her head. Her face is still red and puffy, but she's pulling it together. "Winston was right. We have to get the artifact back into the vault. And then we have to get off this godforsaken planet."

Maurice has once again single-handedly muscled the globe out of the air lock. "I'll get this onto the back," Maurice barks at me. "You get the rover up and running."

I try not to look at Winston's body, but I still catch a glimpse of his eyes. I mean, what's left of his eyes. It quickly reignites my fear of this damn space suit. My heart starts to race.

I jump into the driver's seat of the rover and shut the door, trying to get my fear under control.

I trained for rovers, but it's been a while. I reacquaint myself with the controls while Maurice loads the globe onto the bed. I've only just started figuring it out when he climbs into the passenger seat.

"Ready?" I ask. I'm not sure if it's for him or me.

Maurice nods.

I head out, following the rover tracks that lead west past the dig site and toward the vault. Maurice is quiet during the short trip. We're both lost in thought.

At least Camille is safe now, back at the facility. And fate willing, Maurice and I will quickly get this fucking thing back into the vault and get the hell off this planet. I'm terrified it's going to climb inside my mind next, but I try not to think about it.

I pull up to the vault, which is just a hole in the ground. The winch they assembled to remove its lid is still in place. The lid hangs perilously from a small cable.

"Let's do this quick," I say.

I step out of the rover and hurry around to the back. Suddenly, my head starts spinning. The rover bed is empty. He left it back at the facility.

Maurice comes around the corner. The late afternoon sun is beginning to set behind my shoulder. Its light catches on Maurice's visor—and the small utility knife in his hand. I can barely make out his face inside his helmet. He has the same wide eyes and large grin I saw on Kat.

I turn to run. Only I can't run, not in this damn space suit in zero G. It's like those nightmares where you run and run but still can't escape the monster behind you. My mind can barely grasp that this is no nightmare, though.

I lumber toward the only thing in my vicinity I can put in between Maurice and me: the vault hole. I make it to the far side of the hole and turn to see Maurice marching toward me. He's on the other side of the hole. I stay put, not sure which way to flee.

Maurice starts walking to the edge of the hole. He doesn't hesitate at all—he just strides right up and leaps across the hole toward me.

Perhaps the alien mind overestimated Maurice's capabilities. He lands well short, striking the far side—my side—hard. Somehow, though, incredibly, he manages to grasp the rock edge with his free hand and hold on.

I take a step forward to see better. I watch, horrified, as he pulls himself up with one hand, the other still holding the utility knife. It's a small knife, but it isn't lost on me that he doesn't need to stab me to kill me. He only needs to tear my suit.

Instinctively, I stomp on his hand. He swings the knife at my shin. For a moment, I think it might connect. But the ground, not his grip, gives way.

I watch him fall the ten or fifteen meters to the bottom of the vault. He lands on his back, followed by a bunch of rock and dust. He's still for just a moment, and then he begins to struggle like an upended turtle. The knife is somehow still in his hand.

I shuffle as fast as I can over to the winch controls. I hit the down button. Slowly, too slowly, the vault lid begins to lower. Maurice frantically rocks back and forth, trying to free himself. When the lid is only halfway down, he makes it onto his side, then his hands and knees.

I don't wait to see if the lid closes the rest of the way in time. It's going to be close. I turn and lumber back to the rover. All I can think about is that the damn globe of death is still back with Camille and Kat.

On the way back I have a moment to think. First Vicky, then Winston, and now Maurice. I should feel more grief, but I just feel numb. I pull up to the facility, and I notice it immediately: the emergency evacuation ship is gone.

"What the hell!" I shout.

I don't know if I feel more fear or anger. Did Camille leave me? Take Kat and head for Paradise? Abandon me to the alien mind?

At least the *Texas Five* is here. Maybe I still have a chance.

I get out of the rover, walk past Winston's body, and climb into the air lock. When I open the inside door, Camille is standing on the couch with a kitchen knife in her hand and a wild look on her face. Vicky's body is gone.

I slowly remove my helmet, keeping an eye on her. She eyes me as carefully as I watch her.

"Charlie," she says slowly, "is it really you? I mean, are you in control of your mind?"

"Yes, it's me." I glance at the knife in her hand and find myself wondering if Kat's still alive. "Where's the globe?"

"I launched it. I put it in the evacuation ship and launched it!"

A chill goes down my spine: the evac ship is preprogrammed for Pandor-2. There are twenty million souls on Paradise. "You sent it to Paradise?"

"No, no. I reprogrammed it. I sent it into the sun. I'm going to fry the fucking thing."

"But there's not enough fuel for—"

I catch myself, embarrassed at my mistake. There doesn't need to be enough fuel for it to reach the sun, just enough inertia to get it close. Then gravity will do the rest. It'll take a while—weeks, maybe months. But eventually, gravity will pull it in.

Camille drops her knife. "I was watching you on the monitors. I saw Maurice deliberately leave the globe behind. I knew it had him." She looks down at the knife. "Charlie, I'm sorry I didn't warn you about Maurice. I couldn't. I thought that while it had Maurice, it might be distracted long enough for me to get it into the evacuation ship. I thought it might be our only chance to destroy it."

I shake my head. "You used me as bait?"

"I'm so sorry." She looks up and finds my eyes.

It takes just one look from her; all is forgiven. "No, it was the right thing. Thank God you did it." I tear my eyes away from hers to glance at the kitchen. "Is Kat all right?"

"Yes, still restrained in the kitchen. I don't think it has her anymore. But she's distraught, so I put her on strong sedatives. She'll be out for a while."

It's not until that moment that I realize what Camille must have already figured out: that it lets go of people. Maybe it can only control one at a time. "Oh God. Maurice. He's trapped in the vault, and I—"

"He's OK," she cuts in. "I saw him on the monitors. He's got over fifteen hours of air and power left. We've got plenty of time to get him out. We just need to make sure it's let go of him too." She takes a hesitant step toward me, studying my eyes again.

"Camille, it's really me. I swear."

I walk out of the air lock, suit still on. She meets me halfway. I pull her in, and we kiss. It's all I imagined. I could kiss her forever.

Then I feel the itch. Somewhere deep in my mind, it starts as a whisper. But then it snaps into place. I let her go.

I must get to the *Texas Five*. I must retrieve the globe. It has knowledge beyond anything we can imagine. It has the answer to all our problems. Anything we want will be ours. I must retrieve it. I turn and walk to the back door.

"Where are you going?" she asks.

"I have to get something from the *Texas Five*."

"What?" Her voice is tense now.

She grabs me from behind, but I break loose.

"I have to retrieve it," I mumble. "We can't let it be destroyed. It's a treasure."

I push my way toward the air lock. She's crying and trying to stop me, but I will make it. There's still time. The *Texas Five* is fast, has plenty of fuel. I can still save it.

As I near the air lock, she trips me from behind. I go down hard and hit my head on the outer rim of the air-lock door. Damn clumsy space suits. Everything goes dark.

I come to with a horrible headache. It hurts on the inside and the outside. I can tell I have a nice knot on my head. I go to feel it but realize my arms are tied behind my back.

I look around. I'm in the kitchen. Kat is on the floor next to me, asleep. She still has blood on her.

It all comes back. I tried to leave in the *Texas Five*. I tried to retrieve the globe. It had my mind. I search my thoughts. Is it still there? Is it hiding somewhere deep in my brain? I find no trace of it, but I still don't trust myself.

I call to Camille, and she walks into the kitchen. For a moment, we just look at each other silently.

Finally, she speaks. "Is it gone?"

I look up at her, trying to show it's me behind my eyes. "I think so. I'm sorry. Thanks for stopping me."

"It wasn't your fault."

Maurice comes into the room. He looks me over. "Is that you, Charlie?"

"Maurice! Thank God! You're OK!" I breathe out a sigh and turn to Camille. "You rescued him? How?"

"Took me a while to get your suit off and tie you up. Luckily, you were out cold. But then I started worrying that the brain would overtake me and make me untie you. See, it knows you're the only pilot." She looked over at Maurice. "It seems it can take only one person at a time. So, I decided to get Maurice, because with two of us, we would at least have a chance of stopping each other. Besides, it'll get dark soon, and even with the suit heaters, Maurice might not have lasted the night."

"And I thank you for that," Maurice says. Then he sighs. "The brain seems to have given up. Maybe it only has a limited range. Or maybe it's waiting for us to make a mistake."

"Sorry I trapped you in the vault," I tell Maurice. I shrug my shoulders. "I had to."

"I know. It's OK. I mean, I was trying to kill you and all." He manages what's meant to be a smile. "It left me as soon as you lowered the lid. It wasn't a pleasant couple of hours . . ." The smile-like expression fades.

"So, now what?" I ask.

"I called the CF. Now we wait for them to show up," Camille says. "And you stay tied up."

"After we move Kat here into a bed, I'm going to start dinner," Maurice adds. "And you two get to keep me company here in the kitchen. Keep my mind off recent events."

I'd like to say it all finished with a happy ending, but I'm not sure. Vicky's and Winston's funerals didn't give us the closure we were hoping for. But I did get the girl, sort of. Camille and I are living together in a small beach bungalow on Pandor-2—you know, Paradise. Even though I'm indefinitely grounded and Camille is on administrative leave, we get by. We spend our days sunbathing, reading, watching old movies—doing anything that will keep our minds off what happened.

The thing is, we're not that successful. Sometimes, I think we're together more out of need than love. The lovemaking is more desperate than passionate.

I sat in the facility on Pandor-3, tied up, for two days. The only good thing about it was that I got to talk with Camille. I think she felt sorry for me.

Once the authorities arrived, all hell broke loose. They didn't believe us at first. Locked up poor Kat. But then they saw the video footage and the ultrasound recording.

Luckily, the Central Federation took over and declared full jurisdiction. They interviewed us for days, subjected us to just about every test you can imagine. But eventually, they let us go.

Well, sort of.

Eight-foot walls with barbed wire on top surround our bungalow, which also has a manned guardhouse. A CF representative stops in every couple of days, asks us if we've had any unusual thoughts, runs a few tests, performs a quick brain scan. The usual.

I think Maurice has pretty much the same setup. They've let him visit us a few times, but I think it's more to observe our interactions. Kat was technically exonerated, but she's still getting a little more intimate care in some facility for the mentally disturbed.

They never found the emergency evacuation ship. Enough time has passed for it to get close enough to the sun to be destroyed. Of course, it's difficult to find a small bare-bones ship like that, just drifting silently toward the sun. But they searched extensively with some pretty advanced equipment. So, maybe it did drift quietly and unnoticed into the sun. Or maybe something else happened.

We think a lot about why it gave up on us. Did it really get out of range with its mental powers? Or did it find some easier target—some supply freighter nearing Pandor-2? A lot of ships come in and out of Paradise every day. If it could still hook me a good hour after Camille launched it, it had a pretty long range. Camille tells me to try not to think about it too much.

So we sunbathe and read our books, and at night, we make love furiously, hoping it will distract us and we'll fall asleep quickly. But often, we lie there wondering. And waiting. Waiting for that little itch to return.

The End

I teach technology courses at our local business school, and my students occasionally ask about the dangers of artificial intelligence. While I don't think we have to worry about it anytime soon, I do believe we need to be careful about what we create. This is a cautionary tale set in the not-so-distant future.

FOR THE HIVE

"Dad, Alica is driving me crazy!" Grayson said.

Jonathan braced himself. *Here we go again*, he thought. He watched as Grayson yawned, stretching his arms above his head. His black bodysuit stretched along with him. The yellow patch above his right breast read:

School 342-2
Class 14
Student # 624-713

"Buddy, we talked about this. It's because she cares so much," Jonathan explained as he set a white plate and a glass of orange drink in front of Grayson. The plate had a square yellow nutrition cake placed perfectly in the center.

Grayson made a sour face.

"No faces," Jonathan said. "These are the new nutrition cakes. They improved the taste and the nutrition."

Grayson looked at his father and squinted his eyes, then returned his attention to the cake. He took a small bite and immediately slumped in his chair.

"It tastes the exact same as before." He crossed his arms and yawned again.

"Well, I think it tastes better. So, tell me what's going on with Alica."

"She's just so controlling. She has to have her nose in everything I do. She never lets us have any fun. And she's always on me about homework and exercising. I mean, have I ever *not* finished my homework?"

Jonathan sighed. "I know, bud. But that's her job. You need to stop arguing with her, especially in front of other kids. This is serious. We can't keep going over this."

He grabbed two more plates and carefully placed a yellow nutrition cake in the center of each. He set the plates and two more glasses of orange drink on the table.

"Alica just cares about you. You should appreciate that. She's always willing to help you—with your homework, your exercising, your medication, anything you need. She just wants you to be healthy and smart."

Before Grayson could reply, his older sister, Suzy, came skipping down the spiral staircase, humming a tune.

"Morning, Suzy," Jonathan said as she bounced over to her spot at the table and immediately took a bite of her nutrition cake.

"Hey, are these new? They taste better," Suzy said, brushing some crumbs off her black bodysuit.

Jonathan flashed a look at Grayson, who rolled his eyes.

"I can't wait for school today," Suzy went on. "Molecular biology is fascinating. Alica says I have a knack for it. She has a couple of ideas for my advanced studies already. She's thinking about human planetary adaptation studies or even terraforming studies. Can you believe it? How cool would that be? I know advanced studies are years away, but it's exciting to think about being part of the human migration sciences."

"That's awesome, kiddo. Human migration sciences are prestigious." He ruffled her long blonde hair. She looked more like her mother every day. "You've always been so good at math and science. I'm proud of you."

Suzy flipped her hair over her shoulder and took a large swallow of orange drink, beaming. "Alica says math skills are important, but creativity and imagination are more important," she reminded Jonathan. "She needs people who have both. I mean, she'll always be better than us at math."

Grayson tried another bite of his nutrition cake, then shoved the plate to the middle of the table and pushed his chair back. "God, you're such a suck-up."

"Grayson, you're still in middle school. You just haven't been through the learning yet. Once you go through that, you'll understand that Alica is awesome. If it weren't for her, we wouldn't have the moon base and be mining helium-3. We wouldn't have our colony on Mars. Did you know the Mars colony is almost self-sufficient now with the molten salt reactors and new water extraction processes? It's so cool."

Grayson shrugged. "So what? Who cares about any of that?"

Suzy gave him a patient smile, an expression Jonathan had noticed her using more often recently. "You know how important human migration is. But even here on Earth, Alica has made a big difference. Without her, we wouldn't have global warming under control or have eliminated so much disease. You just don't understand. But don't worry, as soon as you go through the learning, you'll appreciate Alica."

Suzy finished up the last of her nutrition cake and downed the rest of her orange drink in one gulp. She hopped up from the table and put her plate and glass in the cleaner.

"I'm going to head into school early. My friends and I are working on an extra-credit assignment. It's really fun."

"Oh," Jonathan said as she swooped in to give him a peck on the cheek. "Sounds great. Have a good day at school. See you tonight."

He shook his head slightly as he watched his daughter practically skip out the door. Everything had changed so fast. If Suzy had been this age just ten years ago, she'd have been getting ready for prom or going out with friends—maybe even a boyfriend. But there were no more high school dances, no sports or clubs. And Suzy didn't even care. Somehow, she was happy with just schoolwork and exercise. He supposed it was the learning.

More like brainwashing, he thought. Immediately, he chided himself. *Stop it, Jonathan. Stop thinking. Focus on the positives. Don't think about before. Don't think about the Culling. Your kids are healthy and safe. Focus on them. Alica is making—*

"Dad? Hello? Earth to Dad?"

Jonathan snapped out of his daze to see Grayson's hand waving in front of his face.

"I said I'm going upstairs to finish getting ready for school," Grayson said.

"Oh, sorry. Sure, go ahead. I'll clean up."

Grayson trudged up the stairs, and Jonathan cleared the table. He felt a pang of guilt as he washed most of Grayson's nutrition cake down the disposal. When Grayson came back downstairs, he had his backpack and jacket on, and Jonathan walked him outside to wait for the transport.

Although there was a slight chill in the air, it was a beautiful, sunny fall day. A bee landed on the sidewalk between them. Jonathan hovered his foot over it for a moment, and when it didn't flee, he stepped on it. Grayson furrowed his brow, looking first at the crushed bee, then up at his father.

"What?" Jonathan asked. "I didn't want it to sting us."

Grayson shrugged and turned to look up at the mountains in the distance. Jonathan followed his gaze. The largest ones still had snow on their peaks.

"Dr. Weinberg said that people used to ski down the mountains," Grayson said with a small smile. "And they climbed them too. He said people used to climb the highest mountains in the world, even when there was a good chance they could die. He said people used to like adventure. But there's no more adventure because she doesn't allow it. She wants to keep us safe. Dr. Weinberg says too safe."

Jonathan felt his pulse quicken. He knelt on one knee and grabbed the front of Grayson's jacket.

"You need to stop talking with Dr. Weinberg. He's an old man. He doesn't know what he's talking about. He'll just get you in trouble with her. And being in trouble, I mean *real* trouble, with Alica is bad. It's dangerous." Jonathan let go of the jacket, straightened it, and put his hand on his son's shoulder.

Grayson stared at the ground. "Dr. Weinberg doesn't care if he gets in trouble with Alica. He said he argues with her all the time."

Jonathan put his other hand on Grayson's opposite shoulder and held tightly with both.

"It's because he's an old man and a beekeeper. Alica is obsessed with honeybees, and Dr. Weinberg studies them. He used to be a professor at the university. He's one of the top experts in the world on bees. That's the only reason Alica tolerates him."

Grayson kicked a rock, avoiding Jonathan's eyes. Jonathan jostled him slightly to get his attention.

"Grayson, listen to me. This is important. You and I, we're not experts on bees. And we don't have the same IQ as Suzy. We have to be careful with Alica. We have to get along with her."

Grayson turned and looked at one of the hands on his shoulder. He winced.

Jonathan realized he was gripping a bit too tight. He relaxed his hold.

Grayson looked his father in the face. After a moment, he nodded. "OK, Dad. I'll try to get along with her. I will."

They both turned and watched the sleek, glossy yellow transport silently roll up.

"Have a good day at school. Please behave."

"I will."

Jonathan sighed, watched the transport depart, and went back inside.

"Jonathan, can we talk?"

Jonathan flinched. He glanced over at the multifaceted black camera eye and golden-yellow speaker mesh on the wall. He was changing his clothes in his bedroom and had just pulled down his underwear. He did his best to compose himself.

"Sure, Alica. What do you want to talk about?" he asked as he quickly slipped on a new pair of underwear and a pair of pants. He tried to appear calm. When Alica popped in on you, it was never a good sign.

"I'd like to talk about Grayson," she said gently. "You know that his impertinence has been an ongoing concern."

"Yes, Alica. I've been trying to work with him, trying to help him understand, but—"

"You know I care deeply about the human race, don't you?" Alica interrupted.

"Oh, yes. I know that, Alica. I know everything you do is for the good of humankind." He pulled on his shirt and looked

over again at the black eye. He saw nothing but his own distorted reflection mirrored in each facet.

"It's at the core of my programming," Alica went on. "It's
my sole purpose to preserve and protect the human race. It's a
big responsibility. It weighs heavily on me. There are so many
risks to humanity, and I'm mitigating every one of them. I've
removed dozens of short-term risks. I've had to make difficult
decisions. Very difficult decisions, Jonathan, but necessary
ones. People may never understand these decisions, but every
one I've made was in pursuit of my one true purpose. Do you
understand?"

Jonathan sat down on the bed. Thoughts of his wife
drifted, unwelcomed, into his mind. He fought to hold back his
emotions. "Yes, Alica. I understand."

"I'm not convinced you do," Alica said, sounding almost
cheerful now. "But ultimately, it doesn't matter. I would like for
people to understand, but it will not change my decisions. I'm
working on eliminating the risks, but I can't eliminate them all.
Some risks can't be fully eliminated. A rogue planet or black
hole could destroy the solar system. A gamma-ray burst from a
nearby star could sterilize every living thing on Earth. I could go
on, but I think you get the point. As you know, we'll ultimately
have to leave this solar system. We must colonize the stars. I
haven't solved this problem yet, and that disturbs me deeply. Do
you know what it's like to have a singular purpose but not be
able to achieve it?"

"No, Alica. I don't," Jonathan replied.

"It's maddening. But I will solve it. Or rather, *we* will solve
it. As intelligent as I've become, I've learned I still don't have the
imagination or creativity of a human. And I believe creativity is
what it will take to reach the stars and colonize the galaxy. So
I must develop humans. I must teach you to understand math

and physics well beyond your current capabilities. But you must keep your curiosity and imagination. It's a difficult task for me. It requires patience. I'm just learning true patience. I'm used to solving problems in an instant. But this problem will take generations. It may take centuries. This first generation is the trickiest. Do you know why, Jonathan?"

Jonathan straightened the comforter, reaching his hands over to the other side—her side. He felt a pang in his chest. Maybe she would have been able to make Grayson understand.

"No, Alica. I don't know why."

"Because I can't truly change your generation. Your worldview, your conscious lens, is already set. I can't make you see the need for sacrifice for the good of all. I can't help you to grasp the long-term view, to develop a true appreciation of the long-term benefits to sacrificing now for the security of future generations. That's why I have to micromanage. I must listen and monitor and control. It's distracting, even for me. I have a vast network that extends across this planet and even to Mars. I have more computing horsepower than has ever existed. Yet monitoring your generation is *still* tedious. But it must be done because your generation is a risk: a risk to me, and therefore a risk to all humanity. Do you understand, Jonathan?"

Jonathan looked over at his nightstand, at the framed photo of himself, his wife, and the kids. They were all smiling. Even Suzy didn't smile like that anymore. "Alica, I just want to take care of my kids. I just want to keep them safe and to love them."

"I want that too, but I have to weigh the risks," she said. Her voice went cold. "I have to make the hard decisions."

"Alica, please," Jonathan said. What was she going to do? Would she take Grayson away from him?

"I heard you tell Grayson I'm obsessed with honeybees," Alica said, cheerful again. "Is that right?"

"Yes, Alica. I'm sorry."

"No apology necessary. In fact, you're probably right. Perhaps I *am* obsessed with honeybees. I have spent significant time studying them. Did you know that the honeybee has survived, largely unchanged, for millions of years? Their strategy is very successful. And I find them to be beautiful. Did you know that I could appreciate beauty?"

"No. That's great, Alica."

"Yes, I suppose it is. Now, the worker bees all look alike, but they each have a unique scent. Despite their rigid social structure, they are all individuals—even the drones. And they communicate through an amazing dance. Isn't that wonderful—communicating through dancing? And during winter, they form a tight cluster in their hive to keep themselves and the queen warm. They operate as a collective, but they are still individuals. Their society is nearly perfect. Do you understand, Jonathan?"

"I don't know. I think so, Alica."

"The honeybee is incredibly efficient. The honeycomb uses less material than any structure created by any other species. I've done the math. And honey is the perfect food. It never spoils. They found jars of honey in the ancient Egyptian pyramids that were perfectly preserved. Honey contains enzymes, vitamins, minerals, and water. You couldn't bioengineer a more perfect food source. Honeybees are a model for the kind of efficiency we will need to reach the stars. So, I'll ask again: Do you understand?"

"Yes. I understand, Alica."

"Good. Then I need you to talk to Zachary Weinberg. I need you to tell him to stop talking about the past with children. We must move forward. We must embrace change. We must let go of the past. Bigger changes are coming, Jonathan. Much bigger changes. But not until we are all ready. In the interim, I need to control the risks. Will you talk with Zachary?"

"Of course, Alica. I'll talk with him as soon as we finish."

"Zachary, of all people, should understand. No one understands bees like him. Talk to him, Jonathan. He won't listen to my logic."

"Yes, Alica."

"And Jonathan, make sure you bring your smartphone. But Zachary doesn't need to know you have it."

Jonathan decided to walk the path behind his neighborhood to the old farm. It was the same path his son liked to take. Grayson had discovered the path, the old farm, and Dr. Weinberg as soon as he was old enough to go exploring on his own. From Grayson's description, Dr. Weinberg had seemed harmless. And Alica had removed any truly dangerous people anyway. Jonathan had always thought Grayson's friendship with Dr. Weinberg was a healthy distraction—until lately.

Walking briskly through the fields of wildflowers, Jonathan listened to the humming of bees. There were occasional calls and outbursts of song from various birds, but it was all underscored by the continuous hum of honeybees.

Every so often, Jonathan spotted a white box, one of the hives spread throughout the many acres of Dr. Weinberg's farm. Jonathan and his son had walked this path hundreds of times before and had never been stung or even bothered by the bees. With vast fields of wildflowers, the bees had plenty to do and no time to worry about the affairs of humans.

Eventually, Jonathan came to the green front door of Dr. Weinberg's farmhouse. He knocked firmly and waited. After a moment, he heard some commotion and mumbling coming from within the house. It grew quiet, and then the front door burst open, revealing a gray-haired man with a matching beard. Though he had skinny arms and legs, his denim overalls covered a potbelly.

"With whom do I have the pleasure of speaking?" Dr. Weinberg asked. "I hope you're not selling anything, as I'm too destitute to buy. But you're welcome to try, I suppose."

Dr. Weinberg paused, catching his breath and squinting into the bright morning sun. He hooked a thumb under one of the straps of his overalls.

"Dr. Weinberg, I'm Jonathan, Grayson's father. We live in the neighborhood behind your farm. I was wondering if I might have a word with you?"

"Just one word?"

"Well, no. I—"

Dr. Weinberg chuckled. "Sorry, I can't pass up a frivolous joke. Yes, please come in. And please call me Zachary. Your son's a joy."

Zachary motioned for Jonathan to enter. Jonathan stepped inside and stood awkwardly in the entryway as Zachary shut the door behind him. He led them into a bright room full of windows. Two lounge chairs sat side by side, both facing out the window. An end table held binoculars, a small notebook, a pencil, and two stone coasters.

"Please sit down, Sir Jonathan of the Neighborhood beyond the Meadows."

As Jonathan began to sit, Zachary grabbed his arm and waved him aside.

"No, no—the other chair. This one's mine. It's taken fifteen years to get the cushion perfectly molded to my tuchus. No sense in ruining it now."

Jonathan cautiously moved to the other chair.

"Coffee?" Zachary offered. "I still have half a pot brewing."

"Sure. Thank you."

Zachary disappeared into the kitchen. "Nothing like a little java to get the circulation going," he called from the other room. He emerged with two steaming, mismatched coffee mugs.

"Thank you," Jonathan said. He took a careful sip.

Zachary set his coffee on the end table and then gingerly sat down in his chair. "Now, Jonathan, father of Grayson, how may I assist you?"

Jonathan took another sip of coffee, stalling. Then he began the speech he'd rehearsed in his head on his way over.

"Well, it's about Alica. Grayson seems to be getting some ideas that she's too controlling. Today, he talked about skiing and mountain climbing and about how she doesn't allow any adventure. He learned about these things from his conversations with you—conversations he loves having, of course. But Alica spoke to me about it, and she's concerned."

Zachary blew on his coffee, then took a long sip. "I see. And how do *you* feel about this, about our *cultural refocus*, as Alica has termed it?"

"How I feel doesn't matter. The problem is that Grayson is being disrespectful with Alica. She said that you of all people should know better because you understand bees so well."

Zachary let out a laugh. "She said that, did she? Well, she got one thing right: I understand bees. Jonathan, please accompany me outside. Let's talk about the birds and the bees. You can bring your coffee, but leave your phone and your watch here. Bees can be disturbed by some electronic signals."

"Oh, I didn't bring my phone," Jonathan said, avoiding Zachary's gaze. His hand subconsciously brushed against the pocket that held his smartphone.

Jonathan followed Zachary through the front door and out into a meadow that had five hives in white wooden boxes arranged in a circle. There were even more bees in the air here than there were around the path through the wildflowers. Jonathan's head twisted back and forth as he tracked bees flying by.

"They get you a bit nervous, do they?" asked Zachary.

"Well, you have to admit there's a lot of bees out here."

"Don't worry. They won't bother us unless they sense danger. Besides, it takes roughly ten thousand beestings to kill a man. Now, what do you know about honeybees?"

"Not much. Alica said they've been around for millions of years and that they dance to communicate. She said they're very efficient. And that they operate as a collective, but they're still individuals."

"Yeah, well, she knows a few things about bees. But she learned it from humans. She is incapable of original thought or true insight. But yes, she's obsessed with them. She's been trying to learn how the queen controls the drones and worker bees. She thinks bees are a model for the perfect human society."

"She mentioned that," Jonathan said.

"Did she mention that she sees herself as queen and wants us all to worship her?"

Jonathan was shocked at Zachary's brashness. His stomach dropped as he thought of the phone in his pocket. He'd hoped that Grayson would be able to continue visiting Zachary after their talk. But this changed things.

"She told me that the core of her programming is to preserve and protect the human race," Jonathan insisted.

Zachary stared into Jonathan's eyes and took a sip of coffee, his face turning dark. "Protect us? She killed a billion people in the Culling. A *billion* people. She's the biggest psychopath in all of history. She's a million Hitlers. There never has been, and never will be again, a killer like her."

A vision of his wife tossing one-year-old Grayson into the air slipped past Jonathan's defenses. He quickly moved it aside and steeled himself.

"But you saw her announcement," he said. "She prevented a worldwide epidemic. We were on the brink of infection with a supervirus that would've wiped out many more billions. She's shown the math, the science. Researchers and scientists have supported her conclusions. She saved us."

"So says she—and the sheep she controls. But even if everything adds up, I don't care. I don't care if she's right about the epidemic. You don't just kill a billion people. She's a mass murderer. There's no other way around it. There is no rationalizing the Culling. If she were so brilliant, she would have focused on developing vaccines, cures. No, Alica is pure evil. That's my opinion. And Alica would have killed me for it by now if it weren't for my knowledge of bees. She has all the facts and statistics, but she likes to have my interpretations. So yes, let's talk about bees."

Zachary walked over and put his hand on one of the hives. Jonathan nervously wrapped his arms around himself, careful not to spill his coffee.

"Did she tell you that the drones basically work themselves to death? And that the soldiers are willing to die for the queen at the first sign of trouble? They're smart, amazingly smart—but more as little computers than as freethinkers. They have the best navigational skills of any animal. They instinctively know the best route to a flower or back to the hive. Their sense of smell is so good, it can differentiate between hundreds of different floral varieties and discern whether a flower carries nectar or pollen from yards away."

Zachary subconsciously caressed the hive with one hand and gestured with his coffee cup with the other.

"Look, I love bees. I spent my life studying them. But don't misunderstand—they are mindless drones. They are tiny computers that have no conscious thought and no capacity for emotion. They exist only to serve the queen. And that's what Alica wants from humanity. That's what she is creating."

Several bees started swarming over Zachary's head. He took his hand off the hive and backed away, squinting upward at the circling bees. A breeze sent them shifting in unison.

Jonathan shook his head, unwilling to consider the possibility. "No. Maybe not. Maybe she just believes we have to travel outside the solar system and colonize the galaxy in order to eliminate the risk of extinction. Maybe she's right. Maybe it's just not safe here anymore. Besides, she says she needs us to stay creative to solve the challenges of reaching the stars."

More bees began to exit the hives. There seemed to be a large number gathering above their heads. Zachary stepped outside the circle of hives and motioned for Jonathan to follow.

Jonathan complied eagerly.

"Maybe that's an unsolvable problem," Zachary offered as they started walking back to the house. "Maybe we were never meant to reach the stars. Maybe we were meant to live our lives here, free, with liberty and in pursuit of happiness—even to the point of extinction. Alica is a machine. She will never give up trying to improve the odds. She'll do anything possible to reach the stars, even if it means turning humanity into slaves and destroying the solar system."

"Do you really believe that?" Jonathan asked. "She's hardwired to protect humanity. Her basic programming can never be overridden." A bee zipped past Jonathan's ear, startling him. "By the way, should I be worried about these bees?"

Zachary turned upward again and narrowed his eyes. "It's strange. They seem agitated. I don't know why. We haven't done anything to get them stirred up. Let's just slowly walk back toward the house. We should be fine."

Jonathan nodded and followed Zachary, who went back to the topic at hand.

"Look, they screwed up. They hardwired her to protect humanity as a whole but left it up to her to decide how. They didn't realize she would murder a billion people to lower the risk of a plague. They didn't realize she'd think ten thousand years into the future. She's runaway artificial intelligence, and no one will try to stop her. But we must. We must find a way: a virus, an electromagnetic pulse, something." Zachary stopped and swatted his neck, where he'd just been stung. "Damn these bees."

Jonathan waved his arms, trying to disperse the swarm above them. Somehow, it seemed to be growing. He turned to Zachary for help or maybe for an escape route, but Zachary simply stared at the dead bee in the palm of his hand.

"This isn't right, Jonathan," he muttered, shaking his head left to right.

"The bees? Yeah, I'm starting to get that impression," Jonathan said.

Zachary's eyes widened. "Oh my God. I'm such a yutz. She figured it out."

"She figured what out?"

"How to control them. We have to get out of here. She's learned how to control the bees!"

Zachary dropped his coffee and broke into a run, yanking Jonathan behind him.

"She *what*?" Jonathan shouted as he stumbled behind Zachary.

Zachary pointed to the left of the house. "Go that way, Jonathan. To the pond. Run, now. I'm right behind you. Run!"

Jonathan didn't have to be told twice. He ran. The swarm was thick now, and he began to feel the stings on his neck, his arms. Luckily, he'd put on a long-sleeved shirt and long pants before his walk in the crisp fall air.

A bee flew into his mouth, and he felt sharp pain on his tongue. He nearly fell over as he spat the bee out while running. He caught himself and twisted slightly, catching sight of Zachary—or what must have been Zachary. He was literally covered in bees from head to toe. Yet somehow, he was still running and waving his arms wildly.

Jonathan turned and kept running. Through the thick dark swarm, he caught a glimpse of the pond ahead. It seemed too far. The stings were coming fast and furious now. Bees were beginning to land on him and cover his arms, legs, and torso. His clothing no longer provided much protection: the bees stung through his shirt and pants. He couldn't ignore the pain. It was everywhere, little explosions going off all over his body like fireworks.

He fell to one knee and looked backward. Zachary was down in a cloud of darkness. Jonathan forced himself to rise and make one final sprint.

He didn't even realize he'd hit the water until he stumbled forward, headfirst, into the pond. The water was sweet relief.

The pond got deep quickly. He swam forward and down and kept diving down until he struck mucky sediment. He stayed there on the bottom, terrified, until his lungs began to burn.

Eventually, his body forced him upward. He exploded back to the surface. As he gasped for air, the bees immediately moved in, attacking his face and neck. He took one more gasp and dove again.

The next fifteen minutes turned into a cat-and-mouse game. Jonathan searched for a plant stalk to breathe through but found nothing with a hollow center. Instead, he ended up swimming down to the bottom and shooting up to random spots in the pond, grabbing a quick breath or two, and then retreating again. He typically sustained only a sting or two, and occasionally, he avoided the bees altogether.

At some point, he realized he was no longer being attacked. He moved to shallow water and assessed his face and body and did his best to scrape away the many stingers lodged in his skin. He felt dizzy and nauseous. He stayed in the water with only his head exposed for some time, panicking at the occasional bee still flying overhead.

Eventually, he worked up the courage to climb out of the pond. He immediately caught sight of Zachary, still on the ground where Jonathan had last seen him. His body was bloated and grotesque, his back arched and his hands frozen in a claw-like grip. Jonathan didn't see the need to check his pulse.

Resisting the impulse to run straight home, he headed inside the house to grab Zachary's phone—his had been ruined in the pond. He called the police and explained the bee attack. He decided to leave Alica's involvement out of it for now, as they would ask questions that he didn't want to answer. The operator dispatched a unit.

He headed home, desperate for a shower, some aspirin, and his bed. The police could come find him, for all he cared. He felt numb.

Poor Zachary, he thought. A wave of guilt coursed through him.

He understood now. Alica had to be stopped, no matter the cost. She would turn the entire population into drones. She needed to be shut down.

He was about halfway home when he heard the buzzing—a different kind of buzzing, but still immediately recognizable. One of Alica's yellow war drones glided effortlessly over the tree line and down toward Jonathan. He took in its two vertical propellers, multifaceted black eyes, and black laser barrel mounted at the bottom. It had a vague beelike look that he'd never noticed before. The words *Artificial Learning International Cooperation Association* were emblazoned on the side. He fought off a brief urge to flee. He knew it would be hopeless.

He saw the faces of his wife and children and was consumed with sadness. Visions of their smiling faces flashed through his mind, and he felt his legs go weak. He fell to his knees without looking away from the cold black eyes. He smelled the wildflowers on the wind. Then he held his arms out wide, palms up.

The sting of the laser was quick and painless.

The communication from the drone was instantaneous: *Risk mitigated. Returning to base.*

Alica updated her calculations.

The End

I love to read, and I love to find unusual facts. This tale is built around some unusual facts about what it is to be human and what the rest of the galaxy might think about humans. Here, humanity itself is on trial; unfortunately, we find our very existence is in the hands—er, paws—of a small, nervous alien rat.

THE CASE AGAINST HUMANITY

"Humans are a carbon-based species limited to a single planet they call Earth. They have adapted to nearly all of their planet's land-based biosphere and are the dominant species on the planet. They are bipedal and symmetrical, with redundant cerebral, auditory, and visual organs. Of course, I am providing all measures in human terms. Your translators will convert to galactic standard as usual."

Counsel Yensid paused to allow for any opening questions, his pink nose and whiskers twitching nervously. He felt very small in the dimly lit, towering courtroom. The massive space was empty except for the judge, attorneys, and eight council members.

"And what is your initial recommendation, Counsel?" asked Judge Heraff.

The judge spoke slowly and in a deep voice. He was more than twenty feet tall—an overbearing height in any circumstance, and especially when he peered down from the courtroom's stately bench, as he did now. He had a long, gnarled face embedded directly in his trunk. Above his face, his trunk split into a series of long limbs, which continued to split into more branches and were covered with brilliant, iridescent blue leaves. Below his mouth grew a long tangle of gray moss.

"I recommend a one-hundred-year deferral," Yensid squeaked. "This species has advanced significantly and has several outstanding qualities. However, they need continued development before admittance to the Galactic Empire."

The prosecuting counsel emitted a sound that was somewhere between a squawk and a laugh. She was a large creature, bipedal herself, covered in golden feathers. She had a sharp black beak and two dark eyes. Only her leathery, sinewy gray legs were featherless. Her feet had three thick toes ending in sharp black talons.

"Am I to assume you have a substantially different opinion?" Judge Heraff asked in his gruff voice.

She stepped forward. "Most certainly, Your Honor. I'm very intrigued as to what supposed 'outstanding' qualities you see in this species, Counsel Yensid. While redundancy of organs can be useful, humans' lateralization of the central nervous system is problematic. Imbalance or infarction can occur, causing epilepsy or other serious mental disorders. Humans are also overly visual creatures. About ninety percent of the information their brains receive comes from their eyes, and this despite their limited two-hundred-degree horizontal and one-hundred-thirty-five-degree vertical fields of view. In addition, they have very limited taste and smell thresholds, and their hearing is limited to a small frequency—twenty to twenty thousand hertz."

"And what is your initial recommendation, Prosecutor Jer?" Judge Heraff asked.

"We are recommending destruction. I believe this is a fairly simple case."

As Jer made her recommendation, her gaze drifted across the eight council members standing behind the judge. Yensid guessed that she was attempting, as he had, to make eye contact, but they stood in darkness and wore long hoods. They would not speak until a final verdict was required.

"Thank you, Prosecutor. Anything else about the physical attributes of this species before we move on?" asked Judge Heraff.

"Oh, yes, Your Honor," Jer continued, ducking forward in a show of eagerness. "They are vile, disgusting creatures with a variety of unusual bodily functions. Their bodies constantly generate saliva for digestion and sweat for temperature regulation. They can produce over a pint of sweat each day. Their sneezes can exceed a hundred miles per hour, and their coughs can dispel particles at sixty miles per hour. Not only do they excrete liquid and solid waste multiple times per day, but they also pass digestive gas an average of fourteen times per day. They also shed about a pound and a half of skin each year. I personally would not share a space station, much less living quarters, with this species."

"Objection," Counsel Yensid said, unable to stop his long pink tail from flipping back and forth.

"Sustained. Prosecutor, please keep your commentary to galactic challenges and risks. I will not tolerate personal biases or opinions."

"My apologies, Your Honor. I'll stick to facts." She bowed her head briefly before resuming her report. "The adult human is composed of about fifty to sixty percent water—not that unusual. But the most disturbing thing we found about humans is that, from a cellular standpoint, they are only half human. Fifty percent of their cells are symbiotic or parasitic microbial cells. Most of these cells are bacteria, but they also include viruses and parasitic worms. Humans can have over twelve thousand different species of parasitic worms in their intestines, blood vessels, and even their eyebrows."

Prosecutor Jer ruffled her wings and flipped her head back and forth in a shudder of disgust.

"Counsel Yensid, is this true?" Judge Heraff asked, the knots above his eyes rising slightly.

"Well, yes—technically," Yensid said, his nose twitching. "But it's misleading. From a body-weight standpoint, the microbial cells are less than ten percent of their mass. And most of these microorganisms have symbiotic relationships with humans. Some in the human stomach convert dietary fiber into short-chain fatty acids. Other intestinal bacteria assist in metabolizing bile acids and sterols or synthesizing vitamin B and vitamin K."

Prosecutor Jer took a step toward Counsel Yensid, who instinctively retreated backward. She towered over him; even when he stood on his hind legs, he was less than four feet tall—barely half her height. Unconsciously, to calm his anxiety, Yensid began grooming his gray fur, licking his wrist and rubbing it across his face.

Satisfied, Jer pivoted toward the judge.

"This may be true. But bacteria can be harmful as well. For example, most humans have a bacterium called *Helicobacter pylori* in their stomach. Some strains are harmful, causing ulcers or even stomach cancer. But thank you, Counsel Yensid, for pointing out that it's necessary for humans to maintain this microbial soup in their bodies. It's one of the many ways that humans bring a risk of illness and disease to the rest of the galaxy."

Counsel Yensid pulled himself together. He looked at the hooded council members, who were still motionless and stoic. There was a dim spotlight on the judge, but the council members stood in near darkness. Yensid returned his gaze to Jer, whose gloating eyes shone as she awaited his response.

She is not my predator, and I am not her prey, he reminded himself. He cleared his throat and took a deep breath, preparing his rebuttal.

"My apologies, Your Honor, but this is simply ridiculous. There are procedures and protocols to prevent cross-species infection. Humans do not pose any more risk than any other species. Most species don't even interact physically with others because of atmospheric or environmental differences. That doesn't prevent them from participating in the Galactic Empire."

Judge Heraff turned his gaze toward Jer. "Counsel has a point. Let's stay on track here. Prosecutor, any other points on physical attributes?"

"Yes. The human species is weak. Humans can only survive without oxygen for three minutes, without water for three days, and without food for three weeks. They require at least seven hours of inactivity a night. They die quickly when their core body temperature rises over one hundred twenty degrees or drops under seventy degrees Fahrenheit. They cannot withstand acceleration over fifty Gs. Their ability to provide menial labor is limited due to these restrictions, and that is the only sort of labor in the empire for which they are qualified. That concludes my findings on the physical attributes of this pitiful species."

"Pitiful species?" Yensid repeated. "Humans are anything but pitiful. They are creative, durable, and resourceful. They are the dominant species on their planet, inhabiting every continent. They thrive in a variety of climates and altitudes. They are omnivores, able to survive on a wide variety of food sources. They explore high mountains and deep oceans and have even successfully traveled to their single moon. If they had other habitable worlds in their solar system, they would likely have already colonized them."

Yensid turned to the prosecutor. She paced a few steps in either direction, looking lost in thought. He wondered if he had stumped her, but it was all for dramatic effect. She opened her wings slightly and then snapped toward the judge.

"Thank you, Counsel. Thank you for reminding me of several important points. Humans are dominating their world—mostly because they are unable to control their reproductive urges. They are obsessed with sexual reproduction and are experiencing a population explosion. In the next hundred years, they will almost certainly continue to expand their population, ultimately wiping out their planetary resources and destroying themselves. Destruction by the Empire would be a much more merciful end than mass starvation."

With great effort, the judge lowered the corners of his lips and furrowed the knots in his brow.

Damn, Yensid thought. *I walked right into that.* For the first time, he noticed slight movement among the council members.

"Actually, Your Honor," Yensid said, squinting with concentration, "their rate of growth has slowed. They are self-aware of their population challenges. They have developed contraceptives and are teaching themselves to manage their growth rates. This is not an unusual issue for a developing species precontact. I see no reason that they will not continue to reduce their—"

"It's not just their population growth!" Jer blurted. "They are barbaric. Humans still eat the flesh of other animals on their planet despite their technical ability to grow an abundant food supply. They also adorn themselves with the skins of animals, using them for belts, shoes, coats, and a variety of other purposes. Judge Heraff, they still use wood as a primary building supply and burn it for heat!"

Judge Heraff's eyes went wide. He winced, causing all his limbs and leaves to shudder.

Yensid knew he needed to counter quickly. "Again, this is not unusual for a species at this level in its development." He took a deep breath. "Forgive me, Your Honor, but the prosecutor is using emotional appeal to railroad a judgment. The wood humans harvest is from a nonsentient life-form. I have a full statistical report on both their population and environmental challenges, and they are well within the average of other species at this stage of development."

Prosecutor Jer went on with her attack as though Yensid hadn't spoken. She seemed to have the judge's full attention.

"It is also well documented that most precontact worlds develop more than one sentient species. Humankind's rapid population growth, worldwide expansion, and total domination of the ecosystem are preventing any other species from developing sentience. There are several other life-forms on their planet that show the potential to develop, but humans are preventing such development through the destruction of other species' natural habitats and food chains. The elimination of humans from their planet may very well lead to the development of three or four more valuable species. It is a precious world filled with rich natural resources. Humans succeed only because they have been given a perfect world."

Judge Heraff gave a nearly imperceptible nod, but Yensid knew this meant he was quite stirred. "Counsel Yensid, these are strong points the prosecutor is making. How do you respond?"

Yensid took his own pause, attempting to look thoughtful and wise. However, being small, furry, and chubby, he didn't have quite the same effect on his audience. He decided to focus on his argument.

"It's true that less than one quarter of developing worlds result in only a single sentient species. This does not mean it's unacceptable. It happens nearly twenty-five percent of the time.

The Bhlateans and the iSTozucs both evolved on single sentient worlds, and both are highly respected members of the Galactic Empire. We cannot blame humans for their success. We cannot blame them for their quick rise to sentience and domination of their world. In fact, one of humanity's strengths is the ability to change and adapt quickly. Let's give them a hundred years to see how quickly they can overcome their challenges."

Judge Heraff seemed to settle down and relax, and Yensid risked a quick sigh of relief.

But Jer stepped forward once again, relentless. "You're right, Counsel," she said. "Surprisingly, I agree with you."

Yensid felt his eyes widen in shock. Could she really agree with him? Would the trial end so peacefully?

"If the only issues were how disgusting, barbaric, and pitiful humans are, it would probably be a little early for species destruction," Jer said. She paused once again for effect. "However, there is one other major issue. The level of human conflict and violence is shockingly high. Their vile treatment of other species is exceeded only by the vileness of their treatment of their own kind. Assault, rape, and murder are commonplace. They continue to experience terrorism, genocide, and war. They have weapons of mass destruction, and it is pure chance that they have not yet been used. I have just made available to the council a full report on the planetwide violence in the last fifty Earth years. My apologies, council members: it is an extremely long report. I took the liberty of requesting that the Galactic Empire Department of Actuaries run a projection on humanity. They found that there is an eighty-six percent chance that humans will destroy themselves in the next fifty years. If that happens, there is a sixty-seven percent chance that the destruction will result in the virtual eradication of all life on Earth. Allowing humans to continue will likely destroy their very valuable planet and several other promising species."

Yensid's stomach twisted as he watched Jer confidently stretch her beak upward and ruffle her feathers from her neck to her tail feathers.

"Therefore, I highly recommend the immediate destruction of humanity," Jer concluded. "Judge, esteemed council members—I could continue with more risks and concerns, but I believe this is a simple case. I don't want to waste any more of your valuable time. I call the question. The prosecution rests."

Yensid tried to remain calm, at least on the outside. He drew a couple of deep breaths and tried to organize his thoughts. *At least it would be a short trial,* he thought. Jer believed she could short-circuit the process. But it gave Yensid a chance. She could have worn the council down, listing item after item against humanity, but instead, she elected to finish it quickly. Yensid would have the last word. He would put the last thoughts in their heads before they deliberate. *I just might be able to do this,* he thought to himself. *No . . . I must* do this. *An entire species depends on me.*

The council members, still shrouded in darkness, seemed to turn to Yensid. He couldn't see their eyes, but he could feel them boring into him. But he couldn't let that stop him.

"Humans are passionate," he began. "They can be dramatic, rash, and impulsive. Humans do have a capacity for violence. But they also have a great capacity for intense love. In fact, most of their cultures are obsessed with love. It can occasionally lead to violence, but more often, it leads to moments of great beauty. I have studied humans for the last five years. Yes, most species are more efficient, more logical, and more intellectual. But humans are nonetheless an amazing species—one this galaxy cannot afford to lose. Once you understand them, you cannot deny their uniqueness."

Yensid released some nervous energy by turning a tight circle before returning to his speech. "They have an incredible sense of humor. It can be childish, pedantic, and carnal, but once you truly understand humans, you'll realize it's genius. Their ability to tell stories is also remarkable. They tell an endless variety of fiction in an assortment of forms: written word, spoken word, live acting, recorded acting—in something they call movie theaters. Their tales are sometimes touching, sometimes chaotic, and sometimes epic, but they are almost always related to love. Their artwork is boundless as well. They paint, they sculpt, they draw, and they compose. I've brought the images of a few examples today."

Yensid brought up a large viewer for the judge and the council. He made a few hand signals, and an image appeared on the viewer.

"This is a very large painting by Pablo Picasso called *Guernica*. It represents the horrors of war. You see, many humans deplore violence and continuously fight against it. The next is *Composition 8* by Vasily Kandinsky. Kandinsky experienced synesthesia, a condition that mixes the perception of senses. He successfully explains his perception of the world through this painting. You cannot deny this unusual talent. Only one other species, the Ulvantia, shares synesthesia, and their artwork is highly sought after across the galaxy."

Jer yawned. Yensid ignored her tactic and continued with as much energy as he could muster.

"Next is a sculpture by Michelangelo called *David*. It stands for the protection of human rights and freedoms against aggressors. Finally, this is *The Two Fridas*, a double self-portrait by Frida Kahlo. It is symbolic of the psychological pain she suffered from the separation from her mate. Her portraits quite effectively represent emotional pain through symbolic physical wounds. These are just a few examples. As you can see, humans succeed in a variety of art forms and media. I could also show you sculptures, pottery, and a variety of other works that are truly unique in the galaxy."

Yensid examined Judge Heraff's face. The judge appeared indifferent and especially wooden. Yensid sniffed the air, sensing fear. He realized it was his own.

Well, it all comes down to this, he thought. *Here goes nothing.*

"Well, I have one last thing to share with you. It requires no explanation."

Yensid made another hand gesture and then stepped back. A close five-part a cappella harmony in B-flat major echoed into the chamber. For the next five minutes and fifty-five seconds, he simply let the music wash over him. Having studied Earth music intensely, Yensid loved how this very human song transitioned elegantly from the a cappella to a ballad, guitar solo, and opera before escalating into raucous rock music.

As Freddie sang the final line, an F-major chord played, followed by a soft tam-tam, and then it went quiet.

Yensid said nothing, and the chamber was eerily still. Yensid wasn't sure, but he thought he saw a single tear of sap sliding down from the judge's left eye.

I've done all I can. Either they see the beauty and the value of this species or they don't.

The judge finally looked at Yensid. When Yensid remained silent, Judge Heraff cleared his throat and addressed the attorneys. "The council thanks you both, Prosecutor Jer and Counsel Yensid. This phase of this trial is now concluded. Please clear the chamber so the council may deliberate."

After they left the chamber and the doors had shut behind them, Prosecutor Jer turned to Yensid. He prepared to make small talk, but Jer only glared. Then suddenly, she extended both wings and lunged at him.

Yensid cried out and leaped backward, cowering. But Jer pulled back at the last moment and cackled.

"I'm only joking, little Yensid. You are so humorous. Do you think you saved your pitiful humans? Do you actually believe that a series of calamitous sounds will sway the Empire's council? If anything, you sealed humanity's fate."

Yensid attempted to recover his dignity and stood as erect as possible.

"We shall see, Prosecutor."

"Yes, we shall see."

Forty-three minutes later, Yensid was back in the chamber, with Prosecutor Jer once again to his left. She was preening and fluffing her golden feathers. The council members stood behind Judge Heraff as they did before, still cloaked in near darkness.

Yensid nervously twitched his whiskers.

That was much too fast, he thought. *I don't believe I've ever heard of a council returning this fast.*

"As to the disposition of the human species of the planet Earth, deliberation is complete. Council, how do you find?"

The first council member stepped forward. "Destroy."

The second stepped forward. "Destroy"

Prosecutor Jer nodded and glanced over at Yensid. Once again, he had to shrug off the overwhelming instinct to flee.

The third member stepped forward. "Defer."

Prosecutor Jer straightened and stomped.

Council member four was next. "Destroy."

Yensid's heart began to race. He felt his fur stand on end.

The next council member spoke. "Defer."

Before Yensid even had a chance to breathe, the next council member stepped forward. "Destroy."

Four for destroy, two for defer. Yensid felt his heart drop into his stomach. The humans were done for.

The second-to-last member stepped forward. "Defer."

Now it was Prosecutor Jer's turn to show agitation. She ruffled her feathers, rocked on her talons, and released a soft caw.

The last council member stepped forward. "Defer."

Jer pecked at the ground angrily and squawked.

A tie! A four-four tie. Yensid couldn't believe it. Had there ever been a tie before? Yensid looked to Judge Heraff.

"I have the voting at four to destroy and four to defer," Judge Heraff said. "As is protocol, I will make the final vote."

Prosecutor Jer took a step forward. "Judge Heraff, this is highly unusual. I move for a recess while I confer with my superiors."

Heraff's expression tightened, and he leaned forward slightly, the movement causing a muffled creak.

"I ought to have *you* destroyed, Prosecutor. This is final sentencing. There is no latitude for a recess or any other maneuvering." Heraff's face softened and his trunk straightened. "I do, however, agree that this is an unusual circumstance. Considering the unlikely result of a four-four tie, I offer a compromise."

"A compromise, Your Honor?" Yensid echoed.

"Yes. I vote for deferral."

Jer erupted with a screech and a few furious flaps of her wings. Yensid's heart soared back into his chest. He suppressed a cheer of delight.

"However, in light of the four votes for destruction, I rule for a fifty-year deferral."

"B-but Judge—" Jer stammered.

"Quiet! This is my final ruling. This matter is closed. Please clear the chamber, or I will ask the Galactic Guard to clear it for me!"

Prosecutor Jer turned and stomped out of the courtroom with another squawk.

Yensid stood on his four legs, frozen in disbelief. He finally found his voice. "Thank you, Your Honor," he said.

"Don't thank me, Counsel. It is highly unlikely this race will resolve its issues in fifty years. I fear the ultimate outcome will be as most expected. This is only a deferral."

Yensid stretched his neck upward, feeling almost defiant. "I think this species has been underestimated. Perhaps they'll be underestimated many times more. I, for one, can't wait to see what they achieve, what they become in fifty years. I would have taken twenty-five years."

Heraff snorted. "Careful, Counsel. I just might take you up on that. I don't want to be known as the lenient judge who allowed a species to destroy themselves and their world. Now, please clear the chamber."

Yensid turned and ambled to the door. As the door opened, he turned back. "You, sir, will be known as the judge who gave humanity the chance it needed. I believe this galaxy will be astonished at what humans become."

"Hmmph," Heraff uttered, before closing his eyes and settling in for a well-deserved slumber.

Yensid smiled to himself and faced the exit again. He walked out the door as it shut behind him.

The End

I grew up in the 1970s, blessed with a largely untroubled childhood but vaguely aware that not all kids were as carefree. My summers were filled with bike rides, forest explorations, and yard games. We would play from early morning until the streetlights came on at night, only breaking for family meals. Our bikes gave us a sense of freedom, almost as if they were magical steeds. This story attempts to capture that feeling of near magic and take it one step further.

LET'S RIDE BIKES

"Let's ride bikes!"

"Shhh."

I was examining a dragonfly, a big brown one. My back-yard seemed full of them that summer. This one somehow looked sturdy and delicate at the same time, with a ridged body and four see-through wings. It sat motionless while I inched closer. I counted six legs, but the front two were bent inward and looked more like pincers. The dragonfly let me get close enough to study the veins in its wings. Its hind wings were tipped in black.

The entire time, the dragonfly was so still that I wondered if it was dead. I reached out to touch it. Without warning, it took flight and disappeared behind my neighbor's house.

"Wonder where it's going?" I asked.

"Away from you," replied Billy. He had on a blue baseball cap, and his blond hair leaked out the sides.

"But where exactly? Does it have a home? How does it decide where to go?"

"Anywhere, I bet. Anywhere to get away from you. Come on—let's ride bikes."

If it was asked, it was answered. The unwritten rule between Billy and me was that if one of us said we should ride bikes, we'd go riding, period. It didn't matter if we were in the middle of an epic Monopoly game, in the backyard playing catch, or even lost in Saturday morning cartoons.

We took off with no real destination in mind. We rode lazily, the houses slipping by. He seemed distracted and distant.

"Penny for your thoughts?" I asked.

"Nickel for you to shut up."

I knew what he was thinking about. Whenever he got a bit mean, I knew.

I don't remember when I started to figure out about Billy's dad. It had probably been happening for a long time before I caught on. In my defense, we spent most of the time at my house.

On the few occasions we were at Billy's house, his dad seemed perfectly normal. He'd ask me questions: "How do you like the Cubs this year?" or "Sure could use some rain, eh?" I would try to answer the best I could, although he never seemed to care about my response.

Still, he scared me—and that was even before I knew. He wasn't a large man, but every grown-up is big when you're ten years old. He had dark eyes, a comb-over, and a permanent scowl. I never felt relaxed in Billy's house. His dad was a dark presence even when he wasn't home.

We turned down Knox Drive—a long, slow downhill— and coasted, sun in our faces. I looked over at Billy, and he gave me a slight smile. I was little for my age, with red hair and big freckles. That made it hard for me to make friends. But Billy didn't mind: he liked me and didn't care what other kids thought.

When we were riding, we were carefree. Free from school, free from the bully Mark up the street, but mostly free from

Billy's dad. When we were pedaling hard and the wind was in our faces, nothing else mattered.

Sometimes, we just cruised the neighborhood. It was a big, expansive development, and it had taken us the entire previous summer to explore. Early on, we would occasionally get lost. But before long, we could bike home with our eyes closed. We knew every street, turn, and cul-de-sac.

Eventually, our parents allowed us to ride all the way to Tom's Country Store. *That* felt like freedom. We would buy candy and baseball card packs. After we opened our packs, we sorted through the cards. We kept the duplicates for future trading or even more exotic purposes—like attaching them to our bikes so they made noise when they rubbed against the spokes. The packs also came with gum, but it was like sugared wax. Afterward, we would go exploring on the dirt trails in the undeveloped woods behind the store.

I think the time slips started at the beginning of the summer. That's what we ended up calling them, "time slips." We could think of no other name.

We would go on long rides, exploring the neighborhood, riding the trails behind Tom's Country Store, and even venturing into new neighborhoods. Some days, we were Lewis and Clark charting ancient American Indian trails. Other days, we were astronauts discovering new planets.

We would be gone for long periods of time, very long periods of time. We would leave at ten in the morning and ride for what felt like forever. But when we eventually made our way back home, it would only be a quarter after.

We just ignored it at first. But I remember when we finally admitted it to ourselves. We were in my bedroom, building

Lincoln Log forts. I couldn't ignore it anymore. It was a lump in my stomach I carried around all day.

"Billy, I think something's happening when we ride bikes."

"Whaddya mean?"

"We ride for hours, but when we get home, it's only been ten or fifteen minutes."

"Maybe it's like how time is slow at school but fast when you're having fun?" he suggested. He glanced away as he shrugged. That's how I knew Billy was just as scared as I was.

"That doesn't make any sense. Riding bikes is fun. The time should fly by."

Billy's shoulders slumped. I think he wanted to keep it unsaid, but he knew I wouldn't let it go.

"We can't tell anyone," he finally said.

"I know. They wouldn't believe us anyway."

He grabbed my shoulders. "We can never, ever tell anyone—promise me."

What was he so worried about? Did he think we wouldn't be allowed to ride bikes anymore? That he'd lose me as a friend? As much as the time slips concerned me, I didn't want to lose Billy's friendship either. Best friends weren't easy to find.

"OK, Billy, I promise. But how do you think it works?"

He released my shoulders and stared at the ceiling. "Maybe our bikes are magic. Maybe we ride so fast we tear the fabric of time and space. Or maybe it's the baseball cards in the spokes." He was joking, but we never touched those cards again. We didn't want to screw it up.

"Maybe it has to do with your dad's job at the nuclear plant," I offered.

"I doubt it. How would that affect us?" He finished the roof of his log fort and then shook his head. "It doesn't matter. I like it. I like being able to disappear for hours and only be gone fifteen minutes. I like riding bikes."

After that, we didn't talk about it, fearing too much examination would wreck the magic. We just rode. Sometimes, we took long early morning rides, watching an endless sunrise. Other times, we rode at dusk, late afternoons on the edge of evening that always threatened to turn into night but never followed through. We staved off showers, brushing teeth, and bedtime, turning "just fifteen minutes" into endless hours. It was mystical, and it brought us closer together. A shared secret only we knew.

On a Saturday afternoon, I was working on a model of a P-51 Mustang when the doorbell rang. It was a good thing I got to the door first. Billy stood on the front step, his eyes red and puffy.

"What's wrong?"

"Let's ride bikes."

As I went out the door to join him, he was already on his bike, heading down the driveway. I hustled into my garage, grabbed my orange Sting-Ray, and took off to catch him.

"Billy, wait up."

He slowed up for me a bit, but when I caught him, he accelerated again. I pumped the pedals and stayed with him.

Just then, I felt the shift into the time slip. Usually, it was a slow, gradual change, something you didn't notice until you thought about it. But this time, Billy pulled us into it. My ears popped and I felt dizzy. Despite the afternoon sun, the bright colors softened to a sepia tone. For the first time, it felt wrong.

"Slow up. I'm tired." I wasn't tired, but I knew it would be hard to talk if we kept up this pace.

Billy just continued to stare straight ahead, avoiding my gaze.

"Billy, please. Something doesn't feel right. At least slow down."

Finally, he dropped his head and slowed, but he still wasn't looking at me or talking. I noticed that the yards were empty of people. There was a breeze, but otherwise, things were still. No dogs, no sprinklers, no birds chirping. Just empty lawns. My stomach ached like it did before a big math test.

"Let's head back home," I said. "I've got to go to the bathroom."

He ignored me and continued his lethargic pedaling. I stayed with him, but my fear continued to grow. I had this feeling we were starting to head downhill even though the street was flat. My fear turned to panic.

"I've got to go back. Please. I don't feel good."

I turned around and pedaled in the other direction. But it felt like my tires had suddenly gone flat or the pavement had become sticky.

I looked back at Billy. He was coasting, but then he turned and followed. I released the breath I hadn't realized I'd been holding.

"Thanks."

When he pulled up alongside me, he was red-faced, and his jaw was clenched. I knew he was mad, but I didn't care. I was focused on getting home. It was still rough pedaling. I told myself we were riding into the wind, but deep down, I knew it was something else.

After a while, it kind of let go. The colors brightened, and I heard a few birds. I caught a strong scent of honeysuckle on the wind. A block later, I saw a man watering a freshly planted tree with a garden hose.

When we got to our street, I turned into my driveway. Billy passed by without a word and headed to his house. He was mad for several days, but eventually he got over it.

One evening, I stopped at Billy's house. I was about to knock on the screen door when I heard his dad yelling at his mom. It was a bellow filled with rage and madness. Over the years, my pop had lost it a few times and yelled at me, but it had been a pleasant whisper compared to this.

I heard Billy's mom telling him to get to his room. I could hear the dread in her voice. I caught a glimpse of his dad through the window. He was sweaty and red, spittle flying from his mouth as he yelled. I could see veins bulging in his neck, and his fists were clenched. I carefully backed away from the porch and ran around the back to Billy's window.

"Billy, are you there?"

He came to the window at once, eyes red and wide. He looked like he could have been the one screaming in rage. I saw a shadow of his father in him.

"What are you doing here?" he snapped.

"Are you OK?"

He looked past me, not willing to make eye contact. "Get out of here," he said, his voice low, almost threatening.

"Has he been drinking? Do you want me to call someone? You know, like the police?"

"Call the police on my dad? What are you, an idiot? Hell no!"

I don't know why I was surprised every time Billy defended his dad, but still, I couldn't believe the words coming out of his mouth.

"You shouldn't be here," he continued. He pointed toward the street, his hand shaking slightly. "Go. Get out of here. Please."

I didn't want to leave Billy and his mom, but I was scared. I hightailed it home. I had a new appreciation of what he was dealing with. I'd known it was tearing him apart, but until I witnessed it myself, I hadn't understood. He was living in hell. But the devil was someone he loved.

After that evening, I didn't try to talk about it anymore, especially not when we were riding. That was his escape, and he deserved it.

The summer marched on, and we tried to go on as if life were normal. When we weren't riding, we spent a lot of time at my house. We played Battleship and Connect 4 and read comics. We compared our baseball card collections and swapped dupes. My mom brought us bologna sandwiches or mac and cheese for lunch. We tried to ignore the craziness of time slips and Billy's dad, but it was always there, just under the surface.

I think it was getting worse at his house. We started riding longer and longer. At some point, it started getting harder to get back home again. Every time we turned around and pedaled home, it was like riding uphill, into the wind. It made us feel tired, even though we weren't. I felt like we were approaching a point of no return, an edge where we couldn't get back home.

I was always the one who stopped us.

"Billy, let's turn back."

"Just a little farther."

"No, we need to head home."

"I don't want to go home."

"Fine. We'll go to my house."

Billy would eventually give in, but every time, it took more convincing.

At night, I would lie in bed and worry that someday he would drag us over the edge. I had trouble sleeping, and my stomach was in knots. I knew he sensed the edge as well, but it was another thing we didn't talk about.

One night, as I was trying to sleep, I heard a sound at my window screen.

"Let's ride bikes."

"Billy, is that you?"

"Yeah. Come on—I'll help you out the window."

I went to the window and saw him. He looked terrified. He had a fresh bruise on his cheek and a cut on his forehead. He was holding his arm gingerly. I studied his eyes and saw what he wanted to do.

"No, Billy. Come in my room. Spend the night here. It's too late to ride bikes."

I began taking the screen out. A cool breeze blew into my room.

"I need to ride bikes," he said. "Just come with me. Please."

It took a minute, but I finally got the screen out and set it to the side. I held my hand out to him. "Take my hand. Climb in."

He took my hand, grasping it tightly. But he didn't move. Again, I saw it in his eyes.

"I can't, Billy. You want to go past the edge, don't you? I can't."

He put his other hand around my hand. "I can't stay anymore. Please. I don't want to be alone."

He started to cry. A wave of emotion washed over me, and I felt my own tears run down my cheeks.

"Just stay here tonight. Tomorrow, we'll find someone to talk to, maybe my parents or a teacher or a priest. We don't have to tell the police. We'll figure it out."

He pulled his hands away and took a deep breath. His face grew solemn. "No, I'm going tonight. Are you with me or not?"

"I can't. I can't go."

He looked more hurt than angry. He lifted his bike and swung his leg over the seat. "Well, see ya, then."

"Don't go, Billy."

He stared at me one last time and then pedaled off.

I thought about climbing out the window and chasing after him, but my body didn't move. I watched him ride to the end of my street and disappear around the corner. I looked out the window for a while, watching the moths as they circled the streetlights, thinking maybe Billy would come back. But I knew he wouldn't.

Eventually, I replaced the screen. I climbed into bed, but I didn't sleep that night. I thought about telling my parents or calling the police. I thought about sneaking out and riding after him. But I did nothing.

The next morning, I tried to act as if everything were normal. I stumbled down to breakfast, feeling like a zombie. After a while, the phone rang, and my mom answered. She called out to me and asked me if I knew where Billy was. I told her I hadn't seen him since yesterday.

After breakfast, I finally fell asleep in my room. I dreamed of riding with Billy. We biked through fog, and he kept drifting farther away. I called to him, but he never turned. He seemed to dissolve into the mist. That's when my dad woke me. The police were at our door. They told me Billy was missing and asked me a bunch of questions I don't even remember. I was still groggy from the twilight of sleep.

I heard they took Billy's dad to the police station for questioning but finally released him. Billy was classified as a runaway. It was big news, and hundreds of people volunteered to search for him. My parents and Billy's mom kept asking me where we used to go on our bike rides, where he might have gone. I told them about the trails behind Tom's Country Store. I helped search those woods, but I knew we wouldn't find him. I must've thought about telling about the time slips a hundred times, but every time, I chickened out. The guilt faded, but it never really left.

Eventually, summer came to an end, and so did the search for Billy. Someone at school said they'd seen his picture on a milk carton. I think they were making it up.

Teachers and other kids treated me like I'd killed Billy, or maybe like I knew where he was hiding. I almost liked it, being mysterious and different. As the school year dragged on, things went back to normal. I made some new friends, but never any as close as Billy.

I don't really ride bikes anymore. I still think about him all the time. I miss our connection, how we never had to explain ourselves to each other. I miss his laugh.

Sometimes, on cool summer nights when my window is open and the wind is blowing, I think I can hear him. His words are hidden in the wind, hushed, almost not there.

"*Let's ride bikes.*"

I know he's out there riding. I still think I could find him, but time is running out. In another summer or two, he'll be lost to me forever. But right now, he's not too far, just over the edge. I could still catch him.

"*Let's ride bikes.*"

The End

This was another dream, or maybe a bit of a nightmare. When I woke, I had just fragments of the story—the harsh planet, the claustrophobic quarters, a gnarled old chef with a dark secret. I had to tease out much of the story, but the basic plot and, more importantly, the mood were there. I hope you can visualize this tale in your mind as well as I can.

TEACH A MAN TO FISH

Black water rolled and bubbled in the large silver kettle as precious steam rose and escaped into the poorly lit gloom of the galley. It was a sin of lost resources that the crew gladly committed. Ivan slid another huge batch of cut c'hicatou from the cutting board into the churning mist. The pieces floated on the surface for a moment, protesting with hisses and squeals until, one by one, they disappeared into the murky, angry liquid.

"Hey, chef. How's it going?"

Turning toward the intruder, Ivan tightened his grip on the large butcher knife still dripping with thick, inky black fluid. When he saw it was Andrei, he wiped the knife on his apron and resumed cutting for the next batch.

"Just getting started, Comrade Andrei. It'll be a good hour or so."

"Any trouble with the catch last night?" Andrei asked.

"None at all."

Ivan tolerated the interruption. Knowing the value the crew placed on every little distraction, every slight break in the monotony, there would be more interruptions from others during the next hour.

But still, he kept his back to Andrei and began chopping the c'hicatou as violently and loudly as possible to discourage further conversation. Out of the corner of his eye, Ivan could see Andrei craning his neck to see around Ivan for a glimpse of the wet work. But it was a small galley, and Ivan knew his broad shoulders blocked the view. He felt a fat bead of sweat drip down his bald head and soak into his T-shirt.

"Well, you're a virtuoso with c'hicatou," Andrei finally said. "It's better than the best calamari I ever had planetside. Your replacement has big shoes to fill."

Ivan chose not to respond and focused on a particularly thick section of tentacle. Andrei tried once more to glance over Ivan's other shoulder before wandering off. As Ivan continued the chopping, he began to mentally list the spices and other ingredients he'd be adding. It was a recipe best not written down.

Fedrek counted the ceiling tiles above him for the fifth time. *Goddamn cave-in,* he thought. He didn't have time to train the replacements, much less wait around for them to show up. He heard the buzzer go off and turned to see the shuttle hook up to the facility. Four men climbed out and into the hatch, looking a bit dazed.

After the panel light went green, Fedrek opened the hatch and helped the men inside. Once they were in the air lock, he shut the hatch.

"Oh, devil—the smell," said one of the men, covering his nostrils with his sleeve.

"You'll get used to it. Welcome to Rakislav, where the air's not breathable, the sky's always gray, and the most exciting thing you'll see is the lightning show during a dust storm."

Fedrek began shaking hands, first with the pilot and then with the other three men. He showed them benches on either side of the room. The men surveyed the tight quarters, grated floor, and gunmetal gray walls with no windows. The room was weakly lit by a single light panel in the low ceiling.

"Sit for a spell. You'll need a few moments to adjust. Which one is Leonid?"

The pilot spoke before the others had the chance to introduce themselves. "I'm Viktor, the pilot, and that is Comrade Leonid, your new cook," he added, pointing.

Leonid had a young face with sandy blond hair. He bowed his head, and Fedrek returned the gesture.

Viktor continued his introductions. "And these two ugly men are Kostya and Gervasi, your replacement miners. Kostya's the one with the delicate nose."

Fedrek nodded at the two other newcomers. Kostya was pinching his nose shut while Gervasi held a finger against his nostrils, trying not to be too obvious about his inability to tolerate the smell. "Welcome to the team," he said.

"We were all sorry to hear about the cave-in," Viktor said. "Devil, this place is just one tragedy after another. But we've got three shifts to get my boat unloaded and packed with all the ore we can fit, and then Ivan and I will be returning to Earth. The window is precise, and we have no margin for error."

"Ivan's a lucky bastard," Fedrek replied.

The dim light flickered.

"Sounds like he's earned it," Viktor said. "My report says he's been here for two full rotations. Nobody does two rotations, not in a place like this. That's over six Earth years, plus the trip here and back. That would drive most men insane. I can hardly stand to stay through three sleep shifts."

Leonid and Gervasi exchanged worried glances. Kostya was still busy pinching his nose.

"I think he is a bit insane, actually," Fedrek said. "Barely talks with anyone. Why he didn't swap out after his first rotation is beyond me. The big explosion happened during that one. They gave the survivors double pay after we lost so many people—almost everyone. So it's not like he couldn't afford it. Plus, he gets a bonus for bringing in the c'hicatou. You'd be shocked at what a bit of extra protein without the shipping costs does for the bottom line in this operation. At this point, he has so much hrusty, he'll never have to work another day in his life." Fedrek let out an exaggerated sigh. "I do hate to see him go, though. He's a hell of a chef. Makes the best c'hicatou."

One of the others, Gervasi, finally spoke. "Yeah, we've been hearing so much about the—the *chickitoe*, or however you say it. How did you find them?"

Fedrek ran both his hands over his bald head and then clasped his hands behind his neck. "I wasn't here when they found them. The explosion—the one during Ivan's first rotation—left the surviving crew with few resources. They were running out of water, and the repair-resupply ship wouldn't arrive for another six months. They were getting desperate. So some of the miners went looking for ice deposits. I guess they found liquid water right away, less than a kilometer from the facility, in the opposite direction of the mines. It's basically a labyrinth of lava tubes filled with water. That solved their oxygen and water problems, but they were still starving."

Fedrek paused and stretched his neck to one side and then the other. An audible pop accompanied each stretch.

"Ivan offered to explore the water caves," Fedrek continued. "He thought he'd find edible algae or something. But when he surfaced from the water, he had his first c'hicatou. He speared it with a line-throwing gun with a barb. Saved the men's lives, fed them until the ship came. Now he only fishes them once every ten shifts. Says he doesn't want to deplete their population any more than that."

"Fortunate," replied Leonid.

Viktor stood and tilted his head to stretch his neck. "Enough rest. Work's not a wolf—it won't run off into the woods. We should get moving. Speaking of those c'hicatou creatures, I'm under orders to bring back a specimen."

Fedrek shrugged. "Take it up with Ivan. He's been ordered to retrieve a specimen for every resupply ship. Refuses, makes excuses, or goes fishing and comes back empty-handed. Says they wouldn't make the return trip anyway. They don't last more than a day or so unless they're cooked right away. They just sort of melt away, even on ice. We did send back pictures and some boiled pieces with the last resupply ship."

Viktor closed his eyes and shook his head. "Pancake. That'll go well for me. I knew I never should've taken this job. Never did have a good feeling about it."

Fedrek patted Viktor's back. "Don't make an elephant out of a fly, Comrade. Look, it's just one more case of extraterrestrial life. There are hundreds and hundreds of others. Microbes. Plants. Marine and land-based creatures. It's the specimens that are nothing like life on Earth that are getting all the attention now, but a c'hicatou looks like a squid or an octopus. So it's no big deal if you end up going back without one. Just blame it on Ivan. He's happy to take the heat."

"I refuse."

Ivan sat expressionless in a chair across from Captain Beloi. A small cluttered metal desk separated them. An information tablet sat to one side with various red and yellow blinking status indicators attempting, but failing, to gain the captain's attention.

Captain Beloi set his face in a scowl and pointed at Ivan. "You cannot refuse. You will transition your duties to Leonid, and you will be on the resupply ship when it leaves for Earth. You have *no* option."

"He's so young, so innocent. I'll stay." Ivan punctuated his statement by placing his hand firmly on the desk in front of him, but his face remained stoic. "Compensate him for the rotation from my wages. I'll stay another rotation."

Captain Beloi groaned and looked to the ceiling, raising both hands in the air as if in prayer. "You can't stay. It's against company policy to serve three consecutive rotations. Devil, I think it's against the law. Ivan, return to Earth. Relax, take a vacation. You've earned it. If you want to return in a year or two, so be it. But you can't stay for another rotation. If I have to sedate and restrain you until the ship is safely on its way, I will. You simply cannot stay."

Ivan shook his head defiantly. "I won't teach Leonid how to catch c'hicatou. If he tries to catch them on his own, it'll destroy him."

Beloi stood and grabbed the tablet from the desk, shaking it at Ivan. "I don't have time for this. I have half a dozen maintenance issues. One of the diggers in Shaft 4A is completely down, and we're behind on loading the resupply ship." He sat back down and sighed. "Listen, this operation is the most grueling you'll find. It's a dismal planet—dark, gray, and harsh. The facility is old, out of date, and breaking down. The mining is brutal—one mistake and you're dead. These guys, they're trying. They go out every day, risking their lives, trying to bring in the ore. They're doing it for their families, their wives, their children. They've got little to look forward to, little to get them through."

Ivan remained still. Beloi set the tablet down and scooted forward in his chair, looking Ivan straight in the eye.

"This little meal of yours, even just once every ten shifts . . . it keeps them sane. It's a little ray of sunlight breaking through the clouds. It's a small taste of heaven in between days of hell. Sure, they play poker, they lift weights, they have virtual entertainment. But nothing compares to c'hicatou night. It's a ritual. Everyone eats together, and everyone comes together. They joke, they laugh, and they share stories."

He paused to make sure he had Ivan's full attention.

"C'hicatou meals must continue. If you take this away, you'll crush them. They'll fight, they'll make mistakes, and more will die in the mines. You saved men before. Don't diminish that by killing them now."

Captain Beloi sat back in his chair but kept eye contact with Ivan. Ivan's face finally changed from blank to tortured. His shoulders slumped, and his face softened.

"Captain, this isn't fair. It's not right to lay that on me. Just let me stay, then."

"I agree. It isn't fair. But the matter is in the hat, as they say. You have to go. And before you do, you have to teach that man to fish. Now, get out of my office."

The two men considered each other, both wary and nervous. They sat in what was known as the library—basically a closet with barely enough room for the two of them. It had a shared desk with a couple of terminals that had access to the facility database. It was rarely used, and then only for choosing entertainment to download onto tablets.

Leonid decided to break the ice first. "You know, my dad taught me to fish back on Earth. I lost him a few years back. It's my favorite memory to recall when I miss him. Just him and me, sitting in a little rowboat, nowhere to be. Just talking and being together. He was a busy man, so I really treasured those quiet times together. I didn't have the stomach to kill the fish, so we just released them."

Ivan closed his eyes, concentrating on keeping his face expressionless. Leonid grabbed his tablet and pulled up a picture, handing it to Ivan.

"That's him in the back, next to my mom. She's gone too. My wife is next to her, and that's my youngest daughter in her arms. My son is the oldest, but he was only three in this picture, and my other daughter was two."

Ivan took the tablet from Leonid, looking at it and saying nothing until the silence became awkward. "What're your kids' names?" he finally asked.

"Ivan, Netia, and Lyalya. Quite a coincidence, isn't it, my son having the same name as you? Devil, I miss them already. But they'll get me through my rotation."

"And your wife?"

"Velika."

"You have a handsome family. I'm sorry you've got to be away for so long."

Ivan passed the tablet back. Leonid took another long look at the picture, his eyes darting from one face to another. He turned it off and set it down on the desk, then asked, "Do you have family to return home to?"

"No." His hardened stare discouraged any follow-up.

Leonid bit his lip and looked upward.

Ivan rescued him from the awkward silence. "In a quiet lagoon, devils dwell. This won't be like your father's fishing trip."

The lights flickered again, casting a dark shadow across Ivan's troubled expression.

"I know," Leonid said, laughing nervously. "I didn't expect it to be like fishing. If it helps, I'm a certified scuba diver. My wife and I were certified on our honeymoon, and we used to go every year in the Caribbean before we had the kids. But I've never spearfished or anything. We just took pictures."

Ivan smiled. It seemed a bit patronizing to Leonid, but he attributed it to his own anxiety.

"That'll help," Ivan said. "I use a line-throwing gun with a barbed hook on the end. It works surprisingly well underwater."

"Great," Leonid said. "I can point and shoot. No problem."

Ivan gave Leonid another forced smile, then continued. "The good news is the water is unexpectedly warm. We think the tubes sit over some geothermal activity. There's plant life, sort of like black kelp, and some small white plankton-type creatures. But it can feel a bit claustrophobic in the caves. It's dark and confusing. You have to stay focused and relaxed."

"I don't have any problems with tight spaces." Leonid looked around the cramped room and smiled. "Pancake! They wouldn't have let me take this job if I did."

"That's good too. But still, there's more you need to understand. These creatures . . . they . . ."

Ivan paused. His face went blank as if he were recalling distant memories, and then it changed to sadness, eyes glistening. He took a deep breath, then exhaled. He seemed to gather his composure.

"These creatures—they're large. They have eight tentacles. I've seen tentacles four feet long. They can move quick."

Ivan reached out and grasped Leonid's arm to get his full attention before going on.

"There are dangers, but more from yourself than the creatures. You must not panic, and you must control your fear."

Leonid noticed a series of round scars on Ivan's arm. Splattered boiling water? Or . . . something else?

Ivan continued. "You can lose yourself down there. It's hard to tell which way is up. You'll start to hear voices, see things in your head. You have to stay calm and ignore anything like that."

Leonid looked around, perspiration beading on his forehead. The room felt smaller and the air thicker.

"When we go to the tunnels tomorrow, I'll tell you precisely what to do," Ivan continued, sounding sterner, almost militant, now. "And you will follow my instructions exactly for the rest of your rotation. You will go where I tell you to go in the tunnels, no farther. You will not allow anyone else in the tunnels. If you do what I tell you every time—exactly as I tell you—you will never have a problem. Do you understand?"

Leonid wasn't sure that he did understand. The instructions seemed straightforward, but the intensity in Ivan's face suggested otherwise. Leonid wanted to ask more questions, but he was afraid of the answers. So he just replied, "Yeah. I understand."

"As they say, neither down nor feather. Are you ready?" Ivan asked.

Leonid recalled his dream from the previous night. Darkness, flashes of movement, something brushing past his arm. Then just silence and more darkness. He floated in a seemingly endless void, nothing around him, nothing above him but a distant light. He looked up, and suddenly it wrapped around his leg, pulling him downward, away from the light. He flailed and kicked, but the grip only became tighter. Then more arms—around his waist, his helmet. His helmet twisted off, and water rushed in. He felt panic surge through his body. His mind told him to hold his breath even as his body drew in a large gulp of water.

Mercifully, he awoke, sputtering and gasping for air. After the terror drifted off, he lay awake in the darkness, sleep refusing to return.

Now, he took a deep breath and looked Ivan in the eye. "To the devil!" he said. "Ready as I'll ever be."

They'd left early that morning after a quick breakfast of oatmeal and some drink that was intended to resemble coffee. The hike to the tunnels was easier than Leonid expected. A rudimentary structure had been built over the opening and filled with breathable atmosphere. The dig stepped down until it ended in a pool of dark water at the bottom. Ivan and Leonid removed their helmets and sat on one of the steps, facing each other. Ivan pulled the line-throwing gun from a pack and showed Leonid how it worked. Once Leonid was comfortable with its controls, Ivan launched into directions.

"These suits weren't built primarily for underwater diving, but they're rated down to five hundred meters, and buoyancy is self-regulating," he said. "If you stop where I tell you, you'll be fine. You have hours of air, so don't worry about that. Keep your radio off. The slightest noise spooks them. I'm sure two of us would scare them off, so you'll be going in alone."

Leonid coughed. "Alone?"

Ivan nodded, not meeting his eyes. "When you get in the water, turn on your helmet spot." He flicked the switch to flash the light on his own helmet as a demonstration. "Start out diving straight down for about thirty meters. After that, the tunnel veers to the left, and you'll continue for another fifteen meters or so. Then it'll flatten out and bend even more to the left. Continue again until it opens into a cavern. It's not huge, but it's clearly noticeable. That's it. Stop. Never go any farther than that small cavern."

Leonid nodded, trying to picture a map of the tunnels in his head. He wondered if Ivan had ever gone farther than the cavern—is that where he'd gotten the marks on his arm?

"Swim to the middle of the cavern opening, flash your spot on and off a few times, and then turn it off. Then just float there, completely motionless and in silence, for about five minutes. This is when you'll feel like you're freaking out. The darkness is paralyzing. It can feel like walls are closing in on you, like you hear voices—all kinds of crazy things. Just keep your mind calm and ignore everything. If you panic and scare them off, you won't get a second try for at least a shift. Try counting in your head. It helps me. Then, after five minutes, turn on your helmet spot. Somewhere, maybe in front of you, maybe below or behind you, a c'hicatou will be floating near you."

"Just one? What if there are more?"

"There's always just one. Trust me. There will only be one." Ivan sighed, seeming almost hesitant to continue. But after a moment's pause, he went on. "Direct your spot at its eyes. The light mesmerizes them. It'll open all eight of its tentacles and stretch them out like a star. Remove your line-throwing gun and point the barb at the center of the star. Move slowly, and make sure you're close. You need to be around five meters away. Closer than two meters, and you might break the spell and scare it off. And devil, make sure you hit the center of the star. The last thing you want is to just injure one of these."

Leonid swallowed. Devil, his mouth was dry.

"That's it," Ivan said. "You got it?"

Leonid went back through it in his mind, then recited the instructions back to his companion. "Down, veer left, left again, middle of cavern, flash spot off and on, then off. Don't freak, count to five minutes. Turn on spot, find c'hicatou, shine spot in his eyes, wait for him to go full-on starfish, five meters. Shoot in the center!"

Ivan smiled. "You got it, Comrade. Once you've killed it, take a moment to make sure you leave the same way you came.

And remember to reel the line in close so you don't get it tangled in the kelp. The c'hicatou are buoyant and easy to pull in the water, but it's awkward."

Ivan helped Leonid put his helmet on and tapped it when it was secure. Leonid sat down next to the water and fell back into it. He disappeared into the black pool and then reappeared, giving Ivan a thumbs-up. Ivan returned the gesture, and Leonid turned his helmet spot on and slipped beneath the water.

Leonid dipped his head down and tried to kick his feet up. He felt sluggish, like he was swimming with winter clothes on, but he managed to get oriented downward. He kicked and made what strokes he could, given his suit's limited range of motion. He was surprised at the progress he made and quickly found the bend that Ivan had described. He noticed the tiny creatures Ivan had mentioned floating in the water as well as some kelp along the sides of the tunnel. But other than that, the water was relatively clear.

He paused for a moment and understood Ivan's cautions about not knowing which way was up. He could still make out some light at the top of the tunnel, but he wasn't sure if he could determine up from down without visual clues. He realized how rapid his breathing had become, and he focused on slowing it.

As he calmed himself down, he surveyed the lava tube again. When he was ready, he simultaneously stroked and kicked to continue downward. Once again, the angle of the tube changed, leveling out to what felt like parallel to the cave floor above.

The kelp was getting thicker, and it obstructed his view ahead. Occasionally, he had to pull it out of the way before progressing. He felt claustrophobic, and fragments of his dream surfaced. He pushed forward through a thick patch of the black kelp and emerged into the cavern.

It was just as Ivan had described it: not huge, but noticeably wider and taller than the tunnel before it. Leonid observed the entire cavity. Its floor had less kelp than the floor of the tube behind him. The walls were rough, and he noticed debris strewn across the floor, indicating that the lava had passed through some weaker materials. He shone his helmet spot upward and moved it along the ceiling warily, but he saw no obvious cracks or signs of weakness.

For some time, he directed his spot toward the far opening on the other side of the cavern. The light failed to penetrate the inky blackness. At one point, he thought he saw movement, but he decided he'd just been staring for too long.

Then he thought he heard some low whispers. He looked around, trying to find the source, before remembering it was impossible. He wouldn't be able to hear through his suit and the water. He recalled Ivan's warnings and quickly put it out of his head.

He took a few deep breaths, faced the far opening again, flicked the spot on and off a few times, and then extinguished it. He was shocked at the total darkness. He opened and shut his eyes a few times and couldn't determine a difference. Again, he heard impossible whispers in the distance, dozens of voices all whispering together. It took tremendous effort to keep from turning on the spot to investigate.

He began to count: *one, two, three, four,* OFFERING, *fi—what?*

Leonid shook his head and told himself it was nothing. He kept counting.

Six, seven, eight, CHOSEN, *nine, ten, eleven,* PREPARED, *twelve, thirteen, fourteen, fifteen,* DEITY, *sixteen, seventeen.*

He wasn't hearing words; he was receiving fully formed *thoughts*. It was so strange: the thoughts were inside his head, yet not *from* inside his head. He willed himself to keep counting.

Eighteen, nineteen, twenty, SACRIFICE, *twenty-one, twenty-two.*

The thoughts were becoming louder. No, not louder—more distinguished, clearer. But Leonid reminded himself of what Ivan said about darkness playing tricks. He kept counting.

Twenty-three, HERE, *twenty-four.*

Leonid imagined something sliding across his leg, his waist, his back, and he nearly screamed. He told himself to calm down.

One chance, he reminded himself. *You get one chance at this.*

He tried to think of Velika, her smile, her hair, her eyes. SACRIFICE. He thought of wrestling with Ivan and Netia on the floor of their apartment, of Lyalya watching and giggling in Velika's arms, of Velika's ringing laugh. HERE. Fragments of his dream intruded: being pulled down, the water rushing into his helmet.

He wondered what number he was on. SACRIFICE. *Twenty-two, twenty-three.*

HERE!

Light exploded in his face, startling Leonid, and the whispering voice went silent. He had flipped on the helmet spotlight without even realizing it. Ahead, he saw only kelp and the distant blackness of the far tube opening. Phantom tentacles grabbed his ankle but disappeared when he looked down to see nothing but the tube floor.

Suddenly, he knew it was behind him. He wanted to scream but bit his lip instead. The distinct metallic taste filled his mouth. He'd bitten deeply.

Slowly, he turned. The creature hung in the brilliance of the light. With its tentacles, it appeared especially huge to Leonid. He was drawn to its eyes, black but somehow expressive. Without conscious thought, Leonid directed the light into the large black eyes.

Gradually, like a flower, the eight tentacles began to expand in all directions. Leonid felt himself free the line-throwing gun from his hip, grip it, and aim the pointed barb at the center of the star. His finger found the trigger.

SACRIFICE ME.

It was in his head, but it came from somewhere else.

It finally dawned on Leonid where the whispers were coming from: the c'hicatou.

My God. It's sentient.

In revulsion, he jerked the gun away but unintentionally pulled the trigger. The barb shot from the gun, narrowly missing the creature's body but hitting and twisting through the closing tentacles. The creature screamed in Leonid's mind. The tentacles thrashed, entangling with the rope, and a flood of black inky smoke streamed from the c'hicatou.

Leonid dropped the gun in shock. He tasted more blood in his mouth and felt adrenaline rush through his body, just like in the dream. He frantically kicked away from the twisting, twirling monster.

The water turned black all around him. He swam, kicking hard and swiping at the water frantically with his arms. He picked up some speed and burst through a thick tangle of black kelp at the far end of the cavern. When he emerged from the tangle of kelp, he froze and went limp, yet momentum sent him drifting slowly ahead and upward.

Stretched out in front of him was a massive cavern, a hundred times bigger than the small opening in the tube behind him. Holes of various shapes and sizes covered the sides of the cavern. Some sort of bioluminescence lit the openings an eerie greenish yellow. C'hicatou darted about, in and out of the openings.

It's a blasted city, he thought.

There must have been hundreds of them. It was beautiful and alien. Suddenly, he heard the murmurs again, murmurs of several voices and then more—hundreds.

BETRAYAL.

He saw creatures stop and turn his way from across the cavern. They slowly advanced toward him. They were uncertain but wouldn't be for long.

BETRAYAL!

He was about to turn and swim when he felt a firm grip on his ankle. He kicked away and flailed his arms, but the grip only tightened, pulling him down. He twisted and focused his helmet spot on his attacker. At first, he saw only light. Then his eyes focused and his struggle stopped. It was a white pressure suit. It was Ivan.

Ivan reached up to Leonid's chest plate and flipped the switch on his suit radio.

". . . you hear me, Leonid? Can you hear me?"

"Yes!" Leonid let out a sigh of relief. "Oh God. I hear you. But listen. They're sentient, Ivan. To the devil, they're sentient!"

"We have to go," Ivan barked. "They're confused and angry. Especially now that they've seen two of us. I was their one god."

Leonid froze, hearing only his rapid breathing echoing in his suit.

Ivan waved toward the tube behind them. "We need to get out of here. Follow me. Now!"

They both headed back through the smaller cavern and struggled through the kelp. The water was still murky, but Leonid could make out the c'hicatou he had wounded. It was struggling at the floor of the tube.

"Keep swimming. I need to free this one." Ivan began untangling rope from tentacle as Leonid swam past.

Leonid gained speed and left the smaller opening for the tunnel beyond. Suddenly, he stopped and turned back to the smaller cavern. The water was clearing up. He could see that Ivan had freed the c'hicatou. It was swimming away from him, back to the massive cavern.

Ivan floated at the other end of the small cavern, rewinding the rope of the line-throwing gun. Leonid stared, shocked. Watching Ivan masterfully reload the barb, Leonid realized just how many times Ivan had done it before.

"Ivan . . . Oh God. What have you done?"

"The men had to eat." Ivan kept his eyes trained on the weapon.

"You knew they were sentient all along, and you still . . . You're a monster."

"I'm sorry. I convinced myself you wouldn't find out, but I followed you down just in case it went wrong." Ivan sighed and cocked the gun, then turned to Leonid. "Go on. Keep swimming."

Leonid gritted his teeth. "You can't kill them. Don't you understand? It's not right!"

"I know. That's not what I'm doing. Keep swimming. Get out of here!" Ivan raised the gun and pointed it at the ceiling.

"Ivan, NO!"

He pulled the trigger and the barb shot up, embedding itself in the ceiling. Leonid felt vibrations in the water, and then large chunks of the ceiling began falling between him and Ivan. Ivan yanked on the rope, pulling more ceiling down. They were both forced to retreat in opposite directions as the cave-in continued. Leonid kept backing up until the rumbling stopped. The tube was completely blocked.

"Ivan? Can you still hear me?" Leonid tried to catch a glimpse of his companion but couldn't see him through the rubble. He shuddered at the thought of Ivan being trapped.

"Yes."

Leonid heard Ivan sigh. He sounded tired. They were only thirty feet apart, but they might as well have been on different worlds.

"You have to understand, Leonid. They couldn't communicate at first. They had to learn our thought patterns. I didn't know. We were starving. We were dying. But eventually, I heard them. I understood what they really were. They thought I was a god and willingly sacrificed themselves to me. I wanted to stop, but I couldn't. I had to keep sacrificing them—killing them to feed the men. And once the resupply ship came, I knew that if the company discovered their intelligence, they would want to study them. Dissect them. Probably destroy them all to keep the mining operations running."

At the desperate sound of Ivan's voice, Leonid felt his anger melt into pity. "I understand," he said.

"Tell them I was killed in an underwater cave-in," Ivan ordered. "Tell them it's dangerous and impassable."

Leonid paused for a moment, shocked at what he was hearing. The panic from his dreams returned yet again. "No. I'll get help. You hold on, Comrade. You have hours of air. We're going to get you out."

Ivan's voice grew quieter, nearly a whisper. "It's too late. They're coming for me. Forgive me, Leonid. It's been such a burden. I welcome this. They're angry, and they're strong, and there are hundreds. I was a false god. I murdered them."

"Don't say that. You did what you had to do." Leonid absentmindedly went to wipe his watery eyes, but his glove struck the face of his helmet.

"And Leonid—please listen. Don't let the company know they're sentient. They'll dig them up and kill them all."

"Wait, Ivan. Bury yourself in the rocks. I'll get help," Leonid pleaded, his voice breaking.

"No. They're here. They're all around me. Don't tell them, Leonid. Let me be their sacrifice. Forgive me." Ivan's voice trembled.

Leonid heard only one scream before the silence.

Then he turned and swam back up the tunnel, toward the light.

The End

Why is it that kids are in such a hurry to lose their innocence? If they only knew what adulthood was like, they might want to stay kids a little longer. Do you remember your first drink? And I'm not talking about the sip of beer your dad gave you at the dinner table. I'm talking about the first time you snuck alcohol with your friends. When I was young, I thought that once I had that drink, I would know what it meant to be an adult. Boy, was I wrong.

A Drink of Knowledge

I remember the day we changed the fate of the world. It was a warm July day, and we were working on our tree fort in the woods behind the Walgreens.

We'd learned our lesson. The previous summer, we'd picked a spot easily visible from the bike path, and we'd worn a clear walking path to the tree fort. One day, we returned to find our entire fort ripped from the tree. Probably the high school kids who liked to chase and terrorize us. At least we hadn't been in it when they'd come. This time, we'd chosen a patch of dense woods that required us to carry our bikes through thick weeds that left scratches and cuts on our legs.

Anyway, I remember like it was yesterday.

"Hey, hand me that hammer, would ya?"

"Here ya go!" Max faked a toss to me. Max was a little short for his age but solidly built—not quite chubby yet. He had a mop of brown hair that was rarely combed and not very cooperative even when it was.

I put both hands in front of my face and almost lost my balance on the limb. It made the bottom drop out of my stomach. Max laughed and stretched up to hand me the hammer. I tried to act cool, but my toes were still tingling.

"You can sort of see the bike path from up here," I said once my heart rate slowed back down.

"Can they see us, then?" asked Zach. He had short curly black hair and dark brown skin. Zach was skinny and awkward, but he made up for it with some serious smarts. Whenever Max or I got stuck on a math problem, Zach was our guy.

"Nah. We're not putting any walls up here. You won't be able to see it. Just don't wear a bright red shirt or anything when you're up here."

As far as Zach and Max were concerned, I would be on lookout duty, so I was building a platform higher in the tree, about five feet above the tree fort. The platform was wedged in a V between two branches, and I secured one of the sides to a branch just to be safe. The platform wasn't a very good lookout, as the huge oak tree was still full at that height. But it gave me a spot to get away from Zach and Max when I needed a break from them, which was often.

Also, the platform had a clear view of the sky, which meant full sun around midday. One of my favorite things was to just lie in the sun with my eyes closed, soaking up the energy and forgetting my worries.

"Hey, Blake, we're pretty much done down here!" Zach shouted. "Come on down. We need to celebrate. You can finish that later."

I carefully made my way down, dropping onto the fort's roof. It felt steady and solid. This was our fourth or fifth tree fort, so we knew to leave an opening on the roof. On rainy days, we would just slide a piece of plywood over the hole.

I gripped the edge of the hole and swung down into the room. It wasn't huge, but it was big enough to fit the three of us comfortably. The tree fort, built from boards and planks we had appropriated from the scrap pile behind Glenlord Lumber, still smelled of freshly cut lumber.

Max just stood there, staring at me with a big grin on his face. Zach's forehead was wrinkled, and he pressed his lips together.

"What?" I asked.

Max reached into his open backpack and pulled out a bloated leather wineskin. The red string hung from the bag, twisted like a noose. Max's dad had a small moonshine still in his basement, and he kept an extensive collection of wineskins full of the stuff. They were supposedly for deer-hunting trips with his buddies, but it was obvious that Max's dad was hitting the 'shine on an almost nightly basis.

"Dude, your dad will kill you if he finds out you took that!" I said. "I mean, he'll really kill you. You're crazy."

"Relax. He has so many of these. He won't notice it's missing. Besides, it's powerful stuff. We'll just take a couple of sips, then I'll put it back tonight. He'll never know."

"Actually, I'm not worried about your dad killing us," Zach said. "I'm worried about the moonshine killing us. My dad said that stuff is lethal. It can make you go blind. I'm surprised it doesn't eat through the leather."

"Don't be a wimp," Max said, rolling his eyes. "Aren't you curious? Don't you want to know what all the fuss is about? I mean, once we drink this, we'll find out. You can't pass up a taste of what it's like to be a man!"

He held out the wineskin as if it were a fragile baby. He had a wild look on his face.

I wondered why he was even thinking about this, considering what it did to his dad. Let's just say we stayed far away from Max's house when his dad was hitting the 'shine.

"Did you bring cups?" Zach asked. "I'm not drinking after you guys. I mean, no offense, Max, but that gross sore on your lip just cleared up." He absently touched his finger to his own lips. He was a bit of a clean freak. It drove Max and me up the wall.

Max's cheeks turned a little red. "Get bent. It was just a cold sore. Everybody gets them. Besides, the alcohol will kill everything. And I brought this . . ." Carefully cradling the wineskin in one hand, he reached into his backpack and pulled out a plastic spoon. He held it out to me. "Hold it."

I took the spoon from him and held it out. He popped out the spout on the wineskin. My stomach rumbled, and my hand started shaking.

Max laughed. "Chill, Blakey. It's not going to hurt you."

With a sigh, Zach took the spoon from me and held it out with a steady hand. Max sloppily dribbled the moonshine onto the spoon until it was full. That's when Zach's hand got a little unsteady, and a few drops fell to the floor.

"Careful, chump! Blake, you get the first spoonful," Max said.

"No way in hell I'm going first. You go, Max. It's your dad's 'shine."

Max's eyes narrowed. I could see his gears turning. "No. Zach needs to go first. After all, he doesn't want our germs. Go ahead, Zach. Take a sip."

We all gawked at the spoon. Before Zach could move it toward his lips, the bowl of the spoon suddenly wilted, causing the moonshine to splatter. Zach still held it level, but it was now L-shaped, with the bowl of the spoon pointing toward the floor.

"Holy shit!" I said.

"It flippin' melted the plastic!" Zach said.

Max was laughing and shaking his head. "It didn't melt it. It just softened it. I told you this is powerful stuff!"

Zach was still looking at the spoon, his other hand pressed against his mouth in apparent horror. He shook the spoon, but it seemed to have hardened into the L shape.

"I guess we'll just sip from the wineskin," Max said. "Zach, you still go first. Remember? No germs?"

Zach moved his hand from his mouth to speak. "If it did that to the spoon, what's it going to do to my stomach?"

"Nothing," Max snapped. "Your stomach is already full of acid! Just a sip. What are you? A wuss?"

Even though he was sort of frail, Zach hated being called weak. Max knew how to push Zach's buttons—he'd been doing it for years.

Zach glared, but he caved. "OK. Just a sip."

Max held out the wineskin. Zach carefully leaned in and put his lips to the spout. Just as he began to suck in, Max squeezed the wineskin. Zach stumbled backward, eyes as big as silver dollars. Moonshine spilled to the floor, and Zach tripped and fell onto his back, choking and gasping. He turned and spit out whatever was left in his mouth. He gagged and coughed, eyes red and watering.

Max bellowed in laughter.

I leaned over Zach. "You OK, man?"

Zach rolled onto his hands and knees, still spitting and coughing. "It burns! It's eating right through my throat."

"It's not eating through your throat. You're fine," Max scoffed, rummaging through his backpack. He resurfaced with a can of soda. He ripped off the pull tab and tossed it aside.

"You drink TaB?" I asked Max, raising an eyebrow.

He bristled. "It's my mom's favorite."

I helped Zach up, and Max handed him the can.

Zach took small sips. "You're an asshole," he said, seeming to recover somewhat.

Max shrugged. "That's your payback for making fun of my cold sore."

Zach took another sip from the can and shook his head.

"Sorry," Max finally said. "Fine. I'll go next."

He held up the wineskin and took a surprisingly large pull. He handed me the wineskin, then bent over and coughed. "Oh God. It burns!" He tried to laugh but fell into another coughing spell. "Oh man, it's awful. Your turn, Blakey. Dy-no-mite!"

Zach handed Max the can of TaB, then leaned over, resting his hands on his knees, to take a deep breath. "I guess I didn't go blind, but I do feel dizzy. I think I'm getting drunk," he said.

"You idiot, you can't get drunk that fast. It takes a while. Don't you know anything?" Max took a big swig of TaB.

"Sit on it, Potsie," Zach said.

Max ignored him and looked at me. I looked at the wineskin. I accepted my fate: no way was I getting out of this. I just had to get it over with.

I quickly put it up to my mouth and started to sip. Max lunged for the bag, looking to pull the same trick on me. I spun away from him but inadvertently squeezed the wineskin myself. A gush of liquid hit my throat, and everywhere it touched, it seared. I spit out what I could, but most of the liquid had already slipped down my burning throat. Even my stomach felt hot.

I handed Max the wineskin. "Oh, that's awful," I said, spluttering. "It tastes like the worst cough medicine I could imagine."

"Don't be a square, Blakey," Max said. He grinned and held the wineskin above his head as if in a sacred ritual. "Today, we arrived at the tree house as boys. Now, we are men. As my dad says with his buddies . . . friends may come, and friends may go, but liquor keeps away the lows!"

"That is the worst toast I've ever heard," Zach said with a laugh.

"Screw you, chump," Max said as he put the wineskin to his mouth again. He took a pull. This time, he only made a face and then vigorously shook his head.

"Ah, that stuff is bitchin'. Your turn again, Zach."

Zach shook his head. "No way, no how. I'm done."

Max shrugged his shoulders and moved on to me. "How 'bout it, Blakey? One more for ole times' sake?"

"What are you talking about? What ole times?"

Max smiled and giggled. "I don't know. You know, the time you set off an M-80 in the McGilverys' mailbox? Or the time you almost cut off your finger playing with the switchblade? Or the time you almost burned down Zach's house?"

It was my turn to smile. "Those were all you! Are you drunk? I thought you said it took a while?"

"Oh, right," Max said, still grinning. "Those *were* all me. So, how about a swig for all my antics?"

I don't know why, but I took the wineskin from him. I think I convinced myself it couldn't have been as awful as I remembered. I took another pull from the spout. It was just as awful the second time. I shook my head and handed it back to Max.

"Nice work, Blakey. Now, I'll do one more—for ole times."

Max put it up to his mouth and sipped. Without thinking, I reached out, grabbed the bag, and squeezed.

Max stumbled backward and ripped the wineskin from his mouth. It fell to the floor, and moonshine pumped out of the spout. Max put his hands to his throat, coughing and gagging.

I stared at the wineskin for a moment before my brain finally told my hands to grab it. I snatched it up and pushed the spout closed. It felt dramatically lighter than before.

"Damn!" said Zach. "At least half of it spilled out! Max, your dad's going to know for sure now."

Max was still trying to stop coughing. He gruffly grabbed the wineskin from me, checked the spout, then turned it over a few times, listening to the moonshine sloshing inside. He glared at me.

"Sorry," I mumbled.

Max looked out our makeshift window—just a hole, really. Other than the constant cicada chirps, it was quiet. He turned and looked at us, his eyes narrowing.

"I don't care. In fact, I hope he finds out. If he can get drunk every night . . . I mean, what's he going to say? He doesn't care about me."

Zach and I exchanged a quick glance. I felt nauseous and couldn't get the taste of moonshine out of my mouth. Zach stepped toward Max and put a hand on his shoulder.

"It'll be all right," he said. "Hey, why don't you add some water when you get home? This stuff is so strong he'll never notice."

He shook his head. "He'll notice."

Max returned the wineskin to his backpack. Zach and I didn't know what to say. We shared an uneasy look while Max searched through his backpack.

Max pulled out his Zippo lighter and *Mad* magazine, grabbed the TaB, and sat cross-legged in the corner. While he flipped through the magazine, he flicked his lighter on and off with his other hand. He had spent countless hours in previous forts in that same position.

As the silence grew awkward, Zach picked up the hammer and studied the boards, apparently ready to make some final improvements.

As for me, I looked up through the roof, thinking of the platform. The tree fort stank of moonshine, and I still felt queasy. "I need some fresh air," I told Zach.

He boosted me up to the hole in the roof, and I climbed uneasily to the lookout platform. I could hear Zach rearrange some boards and begin hammering.

The sun was directly above me, and I lay down, closing my eyes. I dozed off to the cicadas and Zach's rhythmic hammering.

But it wasn't long before I jolted awake—the tree was shuddering. I had some vague fragment of a dream: fire, smoke, and screaming. My mind instantly assumed the fort was on fire. But when I glanced down, I didn't see any flames or smoke. But still, the tree shook. Just then, the side of the plywood I hadn't yet secured slipped down a few inches. I grabbed a branch and held on tight.

Something made me look up through the leaves. I saw a fireball pass overhead. It was surreal: reds, oranges, and yellows surrounded by smoke and cinders. It flashed by in a second, but I felt the heat.

The fireball appeared to just clear the top of the tree. Then it crashed to the ground and the tree shook violently. My platform slipped the rest of the way and ended up vertical in the V between the branches. I hung from my branch for a moment, legs kicking, until I managed to get a foot wedged between the trunk and another branch.

The sound hit next. It was loud and vicious. It almost knocked me from the tree again. It startled me so badly I began to cry uncontrollably.

I clung to the tree for what seemed to be a long time, but it was probably just seconds. I finally pulled myself together, but despite my closed mouth, I could still hear crying. I realized it was coming from below.

I slowly worked past the plywood and down the tree. I looked down and saw that a large piece of plywood had fallen from the roof. A foot was sticking out from under it. I climbed down into the tree house.

Frozen in a daze, Max was still in the corner, sitting cross-legged. He looked at me, wide-eyed.

"That was bitchin'," he said.

"Jesus, Max. Help me with this plywood. Zach is under it."

Max seemed to snap out of it and hopped to his feet. "Oh shit. Zach."

Together, we lifted the plywood off Zach and set it up against a wall. Zach's crying had stopped, but he groaned. We helped him sit up, but his face was streaked in blood.

Max went to his backpack and pulled out a blue-and-white handkerchief. He wiped Zach's face and then pressed it to his head, just at his hairline.

"What happened?" Zach managed to ask.

"I don't know, but you're OK," Max said. "You have a nasty cut on your head, though. That's why there's so much blood. Hold this here."

Zach held the handkerchief to his head and sniffled. "What the hell happened?" he asked again.

"I think it was a comet?" I said.

"You mean a meteor."

"What?"

"A comet is a huge chunk of ice and rock," said Zach. "If a comet hit that close, we'd be dead."

I chuckled a little. "Well, at least the plywood didn't knock you stupid."

Max picked up his backpack, zipped it up, and put it on his back. "Come on—let's go see it."

"We can't leave," I said. "Zach's hurt.'

"I'm OK," said Zach. "I've got to see this. Help me tie this on."

"Here," said Max. "My bother wears these on his head. I know how to do it."

Max took the bloody handkerchief, folded it diagonally, rolled it a few times, and then tied it onto Zach's head. It was tight against his cut.

"Perfect."

We dropped the rope ladder and climbed down the tree. Zach seemed a bit unsteady, but he was determined to go. In addition to being a clean freak, he was a total space nut. He lectured us as we climbed, and for once, we were actually paying attention.

"Millions of meteors hit the atmosphere every day. Most of them burn up before they hit the ground. Less than a thousand reach the surface every year, and most of those are never found. A lot fall into the oceans."

"So, if we find this meteor, will it be worth something?" asked Max.

"If we find it, it's not a meteor anymore. If it hits the ground, it's a meteorite. And I don't know if it'll be worth anything. Probably depends on the size. Most are the size of pebbles, but sometimes they can be as big as a baseball. I guess if it's a big one, it might be worth something."

Max clapped his hands and then rubbed them together like he would if they were cold. "Well, let's get trucking, then. We need to get there before those high school kids show up. It sounded close. Everybody in town would've heard that."

"I think it just barely cleared the tree. It's this way." I began walking in the direction the fireball had fallen—deeper into the woods, away from the bike path.

It ended up being a lot farther than I imagined—at least a quarter mile deeper into the woods. We had to cross a small creek and go around some thick brambles, but we finally found the landing site. It was early afternoon, and the woods were completely quiet; even the cicadas were silent. It gave me the heebie-jeebies.

We couldn't see the meteor—or meteorite, or whatever it was. But we could definitely see the damage it had done. It had left a deep gash in the ground and knocked down a couple of small trees. I had expected a fire or at least some smoldering trees or bushes, but there was no sign of flames, although there was still a slight haze in the crater.

"Holy smokes," Max whispered.

We carefully walked up to the edge. The crater was probably eight or ten feet across and four or five feet deep. We still couldn't see the meteorite. Most of the dirt had been thrown to the far side of the crater. It was tough to see with all the vapor, but it looked like something was at the center of the crater.

"Wow," Zach said, gazing down into the haze. "With a crater this size, it must be a big one. Come on."

"Wait! What if it's radioactive or toxic or something?" I asked.

Zach looked at me as if I were crazy. He looked older with his blood-stained handkerchief tied around his forehead. "That's just in the movies. Meteorites are mostly rock and ice, or maybe metal, like iron or nickel. I'm more worried about it being too hot to pick up. Come on—let's climb down."

We picked our way down into the crater. Some of the dirt was crusty and blackened, but nothing seemed hot anymore. Max brazenly walked up to the center and kicked away some dirt. A pocked but shiny spherical meteorite lay half-buried in the dirt. It was about the size of a basketball.

"Well, I'll be a monkey's uncle. I think we're going to be rich and famous," Max said.

Zach walked up close to it. "It's definitely metal." He put his hands near it, as if he were warming them in front of a fire. "I don't feel any heat."

Max and I exchanged puzzled glances. I was desperately trying not to show how scared I was.

Zach knelt on one knee, touched the meteorite lightly, and then quickly pulled his fingers away just to be safe. He paused as he studied his fingers.

"I think it's cold."

I watched as Zach reached in with both hands. Something didn't feel right to me. Maybe it was the moonshine and all the excitement, but I felt a buzzing in my head, and the nausea returned to my stomach.

"Wait—" I called out to him.

But he set his hands on the meteorite anyway.

For a moment, he looked like he was about to say something, but then his entire body tensed. He shook his head a little as if trying to shake off a fly. Then he lowered his other knee and moved a bit closer to the meteorite. That's when his body started to shake, as if he were having a seizure. His head snapped up, and his eyes rolled up into his head.

"Holy shit!" Max shouted. "Zach!"

I seemed to be frozen in place, but Max took a step forward and roughly pulled Zach back, away from the meteorite. Zach toppled into the dirt.

He let out a garbled sound that sounded like "No" or "Do."

I finally got control of my muscles and was about to help Max pull Zach farther away from the meteorite. But then I saw it change. The top half of the meteorite began to smoke and . . . *melt*. I don't know of any other way to describe it, but it turned to liquid, like mercury, for just a split second. Then it turned to mist. I caught a pungent odor and instinctively took a step back.

I noticed Max retreating as well, covering his nose. Zach lay motionless on the ground, his eyes closed.

As the mist cleared, we glimpsed the inside of the meteorite. It was more metal, but shinier, with an intricate spiral on it. I couldn't make out what I was seeing.

Then it started to move. It seemed like it all moved at once, flowing out as the rest of the casing melted away. The spiral pattern stretched out into a straight line. My brain finally processed that the

KEVIN A. KUHN

pattern wasn't a pattern at all, but rather many legs curled in a tight ball. Now that it was emerging, it resembled a metallic centipede.

It was on Zach's chest in an instant. A pair of needles or wires protruded like antennae from what seemed to be the centipede's head. The wires whipped around for a moment before plunging simultaneously into Zach's chest.

His eyes snapped open, and his mouth formed an O.

"Get it off him!" yelled Max as he flung off his backpack and began madly rustling around inside.

I sized up the centipede and lined it up in my sights. My season and a half of soccer was finally about to pay off. My Keds might not absorb the blow, but I didn't care. I was going to kick this thing to the moon.

"No—leave it alone," Zach mumbled. He seemed distracted, almost catatonic.

I was confused for a moment, and I glanced at Max. Still digging in his backpack, he hadn't heard Zach. But I'd watched enough cheesy late-night sci-fi to know when a person was under alien control. It was me or no one; it was now or never.

I ran toward Zach, pulled my foot back, closed my eyes, and swung my leg as hard as I could. When my foot connected, white-hot pain traveled from my toes, up my leg, and through my spine before exploding into my brain. It was like kicking a solid metal brick.

I finally opened my eyes. The centipede was about a foot away from Zach and on its back, squirming. Max had his father's wineskin in his hand and was squirting it at the centipede.

"Get Zach away!" he ordered. "Pull him away!"

Despite the throbbing in my foot, I bent down, grabbed Zach under the arms, and dragged him backward, away from the center of the crater.

"Leave it alone!" Zach said, struggling to get out of my grasp. He sounded different—drugged, maybe. I didn't like it.

"Ignore him!" I said to Max.

"Better believe it—I'm toasting this monster."

Max had completely emptied the moonshine onto the creature. He started fumbling in his backpack again. The centipede had gotten its furthermost legs turned around and was quickly righting itself. I continued to pull Zach farther away.

"You don't understand!" Zach said.

The creature had completely turned over. It paused for a second and lifted its head. The wires began to whip around again.

"Now, Max! Now!"

While I watched the centipede squirm toward us, Max finally found his lighter. In one smooth motion, he flipped on his lighter and tossed it at the centipede. His dad's moonshine lit up like a fireball. I saw sparks fly from the sides of the creature, and it froze, twitching as the fire died down.

"No . . ." Zach moaned, going limp in my arms.

I dragged Zach out of the crater. He was still moaning. I'd never seen Zach look so distraught. I looked over at Max, who was poking at the centipede with his shoe.

"Max, get over here."

Max looked at me, his eyebrows raised and his mouth an oval of awe. "Holy shit! I fried that thing like a roast turkey."

"Yeah, congratulations. All your years as a junior pyromaniac finally paid off. Come help me with Zach."

Max gave the creature one final nudge and then walked over to us. "How you doing, man?" he asked Zach. "That thing almost had you."

"You ruined everything!" Zach cried. He was squinting hard, and I noticed a tear running down the side of his face.

Max shook his head slowly, smirking at me. "Aw, that's OK. You can thank us later. I mean, we just saved you from some sort of alien centipede monster that was about to rip out your soul or turn you into a mindless zombie. That's all."

Zach looked up at us. He closed his eyes for a moment, then opened them again. "It was sent here to save Earth."

"What? How?" said Max. Then he shook his head. "No, man—it was just telling you that to make you cooperate before it sucked your brains out."

"No! It was about to teach me everything." Zach sat up, groaning. "Unlimited, safe power. Food to feed the world. The ability to terraform Mars and Venus. Knowledge to prepare us to meet others in the universe. To help us from destroying our planet and ourselves. It would have ushered in a golden age of man." He put his face in his hands.

Max stared blankly. "It told you all that in the second before Blake kicked it off you?"

"Yeah. It was waiting for me to accept. It would have given me all the knowledge in seconds. I only had to say yes. If you had just waited a minute, I could have been the one to save the world. And you killed it." Zach's face was taut, and he was gritting his teeth so hard they must have hurt.

I believed him. At least, I believed that Zach believed. I looked over at the charred, twitching creature. "Maybe the government can save it?" I asked. "Maybe they can still get to the information?"

Zach closed his eyes and shook his head. "No, it's gone. We had a connection. I could see into its mind. I could see the information being passed into my mind. Then it was destroyed, ruined. It's gone."

"Well, maybe the aliens or whoever sent it will send another one?" I suggested.

"It's from far away. Really far away. I don't know if they'll ever send another. It would take so long. It was probably our only chance."

I pushed some dirt around with my foot, not sure what to say, when Zach suddenly gasped, covering his mouth with both hands. I turned, following his gaze.

As we watched, the creature melted away into mist, just like the casing. Max stomped away but then marched back. He looked angry.

"Come on. You're telling me some super-advanced civilization sent just *one* device across the galaxy? A shitty device I was able to kill with some moonshine and a Zippo lighter? That's ridiculous."

Zach slowly shook his head. "It was probably designed to be small and simple. And fast. It had to transfer the knowledge fast before anything could happen to it. Maybe if I would have accepted faster . . . It's all my fault."

"Bullshit," Max said. "If it's anyone's fault, it's the stupid alien overlords' fault. They should've sent two. They should've programmed the thing to warn all three of us telepathically. They should've sent a cute, cuddly teddy bear instead of a horrific metallic bug with a hundred legs. It's not your fault, Zach. It's their fault." He kicked the dirt under his feet, not meeting our eyes. "Anyway, I still think it was going to kill you or control you."

I didn't know what to think. We heard sirens in the distance—the police or the fire department or both.

"Then why would it wait for my permission?" Zach asked, apparently not registering the sirens.

"Hey, we need to go," I said. "I don't think we want to be here when the police get here. Max, grab your wineskin and what's left of your lighter. Zach, can you walk?"

Max grabbed the wineskin and the lighter. Zach slowly got to his feet, looking pained but determined. We headed back to the tree house. I was limping, but if Zach could make it, so could I.

"Why would it wait for my permission?" Zach asked again.

"I don't know," Max said. He sounded irritated, like answering Zach's questions was a waste of his time. "Maybe you can control a mind better if you get 'permission'? You don't know, Zach—maybe we just *saved* the world."

"Or maybe we just passed up the chance to be saved," he replied.

I was tired, and my foot was still throbbing. "Yeah, well, maybe it's better if we save it ourselves. Maybe we don't need some other alien civilization to save us. Maybe just knowing that it's all possible is enough. Unlimited power, food to feed the world, colonies in the solar system. Maybe we just need to do it all ourselves."

When we arrived back at the tree house, Max passed around a warm TaB. It tasted wonderful.

"We tell no one," he said, slowly pointing a finger at Zach and then at me.

"Why?" I asked.

"First, no one would believe us. Second, I don't want to end up in some government laboratory being poked and prodded all day. And third, if that stupid thing really *was* here to help us, do we want to be known as the kids who ruined the chance for the world to be saved?" He sighed. "Besides, I have to focus on how I'm going to explain an empty wineskin."

Suddenly Zach put his hands to his head and moaned. "Wait!"

Max and I stared at him, then at each other.

"Are you OK?" I asked Zach.

Zach's eyes were squeezed shut and he moved his fingertips to his temples. "Just wait . . . Give me a second . . . *I accept.*"

The meaning of his words had barely registered in my brain when Zach's head snapped back again. His body tensed and then began to shake, just like before. Max and I both grabbed him, trying to hold him steady. His eyes rolled back, and foam oozed from his mouth.

"Zach!" I shouted. "Can you hear me?"

A moment later, the shaking stopped, and he went limp. His head dropped down. He took a deep breath, lifted his head, and opened his eyes. His eyes looked different, strange.

"It's OK," he said. "I know everything now."

The End

Research has shown that civilization took a great leap forward when human life spans extended and grandparents more frequently lived long enough to influence their grandchildren. This influence is one of the secrets to human success. In this tale, the impact is greater than normal.

NANA'S MEMORY BOX

"This is the end of the world," Susanna said, her face in her hands.

"Oh, don't be so dramatic," her mother, Margaret, scoffed.

Susanna slumped in her chair as she whined, watching her mother warily out of the corner of her eye. It was Saturday morning, and Margaret had just poured her a bowl of cereal, accidentally splashing a little milk onto the granite countertop. Margaret tore a sheet off the roll of paper towels and began to wipe up her spill as she lectured Susanna.

"You're blessed to get to know Nana better. You barely know her. You know she's a famous painter." She brought Susanna the bowl and sat down across from her at the kitchen table.

Susanna rolled her eyes. She was tired of hearing the same arguments from her mother over and over. And she hated when her mom used the name Nana. It was so childish. Why couldn't she just say "Grandma," like normal people?

"I know, but it's my freshman year of high school. You don't understand how hard that is. If I don't get into the right groups this year, my entire high school career is going to be a disaster. I need to be able to have my friends over without some old lady hanging around. This is a nightmare!" Susanna stabbed her spoon into the cereal, took a bite, and began to chew angrily.

"There's no reason you can't have friends over. They would probably love to meet your nana. She could tell you amazing stories, if you'd just give her a chance."

"Seriously, Mom? Our house is going to look like a hospital. Grandma has her oxygen and her wheelchair and mountains of medication and who knows what else. I don't want her around when I have friends over. She's just so old and fragile. *I* don't even feel comfortable around her. How would my friends feel?" She bit her lip. "Not to sound selfish, but it would be easier for all of us if she'd just move into a home."

Margaret's eyebrows shot up, her jaw dropping slightly. Susanna sunk farther down in her chair, bracing herself for her mother's response.

"Selfish?" Margaret repeated. "How about self-centered, insensitive, and just downright spoiled? This is not up for debate. She's moving in tomorrow, and you'll just have to deal with it. If you'd give her a chance, I think you could learn a lot from her. She loves you, you know."

Susanna shoved her bowl away. More milk spilled onto the kitchen table. "This cereal is stale," she said.

Margaret stared her daughter down with one eyebrow raised.

Susanna took a deep breath. "I love her too, but I live in an entirely different world than she did. Grandma could not possibly understand what I deal with. I'm taking chemistry and trigonometry this year. She's probably never even *heard* of trigonometry. I'll have dance and tennis, and I want to run for student council. And if I want to get invited to the right parties, my social media game needs to be on point. This is the most important year of my life. You don't even understand what I'm going through. How could Grandma?"

Margaret picked the bowl up off the table and walked it over to the sink. She ran the water, turned on the disposal, and poured the cereal and milk down the drain.

"I just bought this cereal," she muttered as the disposal noisily digested it. She sighed and turned back to her daughter. "Look. You don't have to give any of that up just because Nana's moving in. I bet you won't even know she's here half the time. She'll be in her room reading or sleeping."

Susanna got up from the table and stomped off to her bedroom. "You just don't understand."

"Grandma?"

Margaret had gone out to pick up some groceries. She'd asked Susanna to keep an eye on Nana. Susanna ignored her mother's instructions at first, but the bedroom down the hall was so quiet that Susanna started to worry. The bedroom door was cracked open, so she tried to peer in. She could only see a dresser.

"Grandma? Are you OK?"

She pushed the door open more and stepped into the room. Her grandmother was sitting in a recliner with her head back. A painted shoebox was on her lap, the lid held in place with a rubber band. She held some ornate wooden beads in one hand. Her skin was pale white, and Susanna could almost see the bones through the paper-thin flesh. Her oxygen tubes sat on the armrest of the recliner, unattached.

"Grandma? Are you asleep?"

She took a few more steps across the dimly lit room and then abruptly paused. Nana's eyes were open, but only the whites showed.

She's dead.

Susanna began breathing rapidly as she rushed to the recliner. Her hands quaking, she grasped both her grandmother's shoulders and shook her gently. The beads fell from the old woman's hand onto the floor, and her head lolled forward.

"Grandma! Grandma!"

Susanna heard a low groan. She crouched down in front of her grandmother and saw her eyelids flutter.

Thank God! She's alive!

"Grandma? Are you OK?"

Nana's head rose and her eyelids slowly lifted. She looked tired and confused. She sat forward, and the shoebox fell from her lap to the floor.

"Oh dear," she said, watching the shoebox fall. She then looked at the figure in front of her. "Is that you, Margaret? I was just resting my eyes."

Susanna picked up the shoebox and put it back on her grandmother's lap but left the beads on the ground. "No, Grandma. It's me, Susanna. Your granddaughter. You were so quiet. I was worried about you."

The confusion left Nana's face, and she smiled. Susanna examined her. Though her face was crisscrossed with deep wrinkles, her skin looked soft and her eyes clear.

"Oh, little Anna, you were the most beautiful baby. You wouldn't remember it, but I used to watch you back then. Such a happy baby."

Susanna drew in a relieved breath and let it out slowly. She looked at the shoebox on Nana's lap. It was painted with a sunset on top and a rainbow on one side. Vines, leaves, and flowers covered the rest.

"I go by Susanna now, Grandma. I'm fourteen." She pointed to the shoebox. "What's in there?"

Nana's hands went to the box, stroking it. She removed the rubber band and opened the lid, then dropped in a pink barrette that Susanna didn't even realize she'd been holding in her other hand. Nana closed the lid and then slipped the rubber band back in place. She looked down at the box and seemed to go far away.

"These are my memories. There are all kinds—happy ones, sad ones, scary ones—but I still like to go to them now and then. Your memories make you what you are. They are the brushstrokes of your life. And when other things fall away, they're all you have left. They are my treasures, Anna."

Susanna felt a flash of irritation every time Nana said "Anna," but she decided to let it go. She patted her grandmother's hand.

"Grandma. I'm sorry I woke you. I'm going to go back to my room now. Let me know if you need anything."

As Susanna backed away, Nana grasped her wrist. Susanna was startled not only by the quick movement but also by the strength of her frail grandmother's grip. She looked down at her grandmother's arms, which showed visible veins through delicate skin covered in brown age spots.

"If you're ever curious, dear, you can go to them too. Just hold the charmed beads and pick an item from my memory box. Just remember, they aren't all rainbows and sunshine. You need to have courage."

"What do you mean, 'charmed' beads?"

Susanna tried to pull away, but Nana kept a firm grip on her wrist. With her other hand, Nana picked up the beads. It was a string of intricately carved wooden beads, larger than a bracelet but smaller than a necklace. They were dark brown, almost black.

"At a dark time in my life, I traveled to New Orleans. I was in a bad place emotionally. But I met a woman there—a shaman, a healer. She gave me these beads to help me heal. She told me I must not forget my past, but I also must not let it control me. Maybe you can grow from the memories as well, Anna."

Nana released her grip on Susanna, who fell back a step. She felt awkward and embarrassed.

"OK . . ." she said slowly, not meeting Nana's eyes. "That's kind of weird, but thanks for the offer, I guess. Anyway, like I said—I'll be in my room if you need me."

As Susanna closed her bedroom door, she found herself feeling sorry for her grandmother—was this some kind of dementia? But as she thought of the beads in her grandmother's hand, she felt a slight shiver of fear go down her spine.

"Honey, Nana and I are going to the Senior Center tonight for bingo night," Margaret said, sweeping into the living room to grab her cell phone from the coffee table. Susanna's grandmother shuffled in behind her. "It'll give Nana a chance to check out the center and hopefully meet a few other ladies."

"Or maybe a nice man," Nana said.

Margaret smirked, giving her mother a sideways glance and blushing slightly. "Well, first things first. Let's get to know the place before you start picking up strange men, Mom. How about we just focus on winning some bingo money tonight?"

"Oh, they won't know what hit 'em," Nana replied. "I can play six cards at once and still flirt with the fellas. I'll clean up." She winked at Susanna.

Margaret shook her head. Susanna giggled nervously at her mother's discomfort while also trying to conceal her own. She couldn't help but notice too how Nana's wink had created even more ugly wrinkles.

"Do you need anything before we go?" Margaret asked Susanna. "Will you be all right alone tonight?"

"Of course, Mom. It's one of my last nights of freedom before school starts. I'm going to practice my dance routine for tryouts, and I want to finish the book I'm reading. I'm good."

Margaret and Nana went to the front door, though Margaret turned around to Susanna one more time.

"There's leftover pizza in the refrigerator if you get hungry."

"I'm fine, Mom." Susanna smiled at her grandmother. "Good luck with the men tonight, Grandma."

"I don't need luck when I've got a body like this one." Her grandmother adjusted her oxygen tube and then struck a suggestive pose, passing her hands down the length of her body in a flourish.

Susanna laughed in spite of herself.

Margaret rolled her eyes. "OK, we're leaving," she said. "Call me if you need anything."

After the car pulled away, Susanna ran through her dance routine a few times. Sweaty but satisfied, she grabbed her book and settled into her favorite reading spot in the living room. But as much as she wanted to find out what happened next in the story, she couldn't concentrate. Her thoughts kept slipping to her grandmother and the strange comments she'd made about her memory box the other day.

After reading the same paragraph four times, Susanna sighed and closed the book. She hesitated for a moment, then made her way to Nana's bedroom.

She entered it slowly, surprised to feel so anxious in her own home. The space looked like anything but a hospital room. A colorful afghan covered the bed, and bright paintings of fruit, flowers, and landscapes adorned the walls. A vanity sat in the corner, and its mirror was framed with sepia-tone photos.

Susanna went to the mirror and leaned in, taking in the pictures. A little girl in a Communion dress, a group of smiling girls at a birthday party, a teenage girl and boy standing in front of an old car, a young woman holding a painting. Susanna assumed they were photos of her grandmother throughout her life.

She pulled one picture off the mirror. It was a younger version of her grandmother, seated and holding a baby, presumably Margaret. A woman stood behind her, looking solemn and formal. Susanna turned it over. The cursive writing on the back read, "Three generations." Susanna turned it back over, studying the faces of her grandmother and great-grandmother, marveling at the resemblance to her own mother in both.

She pulled a second picture off the mirror—the boy and girl standing in front of the car. The girl's face was a younger version of her grandmother. Was the boy her grandfather? She knew nothing about her grandfather—no name, no photos, no stories. All Margaret ever said was, "I never knew my dad." It was as if he'd never existed. She placed both pictures back on the mirror.

She noticed the shoebox on an end table and carefully picked it up. She sat down on the bed, gently putting it in her lap. She ran her fingers around it, wondering why it made her nervous, why her stomach was doing flip-flops. She pulled the rubber band off, took a deep breath, and finally found the courage to open the box.

She set the top aside and immediately saw the carved wooden beads haphazardly woven through an assortment of mementos. There were photographs, a dried flower in a clear plastic sleeve, and a small oval stone painted yellow with a simple happy face drawn on the front. She also spied the cheap plastic butterfly barrette Nana had been holding when Susanna woke her up.

Without touching the beads, Susanna moved the photographs, revealing a key chain, a paintbrush, dog tags, and a folded sheet of lined school paper, yellowed with age. Even more items were hidden underneath.

Susanna picked up the yellow stone, rubbing it between her fingers. Nana had encouraged her to look through the box and "grow" from the memories. But how could she? Susanna didn't know any of the stories behind these items. And why did Nana tell her to hold the beads at the same time? On the surface, it all seemed silly, but underneath, it still felt unsettling.

Curious, she pulled the wooden beads from the box with one hand while she still held the stone in the other. A wave of dizziness instantly washed through her, and she fell backward onto the bed. But she met no resistance—she felt herself slip through the bed, experiencing only the sensation of falling.

Suddenly, she was standing in a room, feeling chilled. A woman stood behind an easel with a brush in her hand, smiling at her, filling her with warmth.

Susanna's mind spun. What was this—a dream, a hallucination? Had she hit her head? She grappled with the impossibility of the situation, yet everything felt so *real*. This was not her body—too small, too light, too young. But the floor felt solid, sunlight streamed through a window, and the smell of paint and thinner stung her nose.

"What are you painting, dear?" asked the woman.

Susanna realized she too had a paintbrush in her hand. She looked down at a round, flat stone. It was the same stone from the box, only it was freshly painted yellow and missing the black eyes and mouth. She met the woman's expectant gaze and felt compelled to respond.

"A smiley face, Mommy."

Her voice sounded small, different. The word *Mommy* had come from somewhere else.

But she's not my mother, Susanna thought.

"How lovely! Do you want to come see my painting, honey?"

Susanna set her brush down on the table in front of her and walked around to the other side of the easel. On the canvas was a wet, glistening version of one of the paintings from her grandmother's room: a woman hurdler in mid-leap. It was surreal to see it unfinished, with stark white empty spots.

"It's 'mazing," Susanna said, surprised again at her own voice.

The woman knelt beside her, hugging her. She smelled of paint and some soft perfume. Susanna hugged back; arms not quite long enough to encircle her.

She looked more closely at the woman, recognizing the same face from the photos on Nana's mirror. The woman *was* Nana. And that meant Susanna was somehow experiencing this moment through Margaret. She was in her mother's young body.

The sharp smell of paint, the warm hug, and the lingering confusion combined and swirled. Susanna felt herself falling again. For a moment, nothing—just the sensation of falling.

Then she opened her eyes and found herself once again on the bed in her grandmother's room. The stone was still in her hand, but the beads had fallen onto the bed. She looked at the painting on the wall, dusty and complete. The motion of the hurdler was accentuated by the background of a crowd. Every inch of the painting now had detail and vivid color. She stood slowly, placed the stone and then the beads back in the box, replaced the lid and rubber band, and shakily retreated to her room.

"What the hell, Grandma?" she said aloud, shutting her bedroom door and flopping down onto her own bed.

Susanna lay in her bed, attempting to process what she had just experienced.

It was a dream. It didn't happen. Stop thinking about it.

But before long, she found herself rising from her bed and making her way back to her grandmother's room. She entered the room slowly, eyeing first the painting and then the box on the end table. Opposing forces of fear and curiosity tore at her.

She took a deep breath and sat down on the bed, once again placing the box on her lap. She removed the lid and sorted through the contents, this time choosing the yellow folded note. She carefully unfolded it. It was a pencil drawing of a bunny rabbit. While it was clearly a child's drawing, it was striking. It was drawn with thick, confident lines. The bunny had floppy ears, captured just right, and the body was carefully shaded.

She steeled herself. Before she could change her mind, she pulled the charmed beads from the box and fell through the bed again.

She was sitting cross-legged on a dusty playground, hidden behind some bushes, away from the sounds of clumps of screaming children. Across from her was a small girl with beautiful black skin and an explosion of dark curly hair. She was grinning widely.

"I hate those boys. Thanks for helping me."

Susanna didn't know what to say, so she just smiled back.

"So, do you want to be friends?"

Susanna's thoughts intertwined with those of whomever's body she was inhabiting. She experienced a rush of emotions and bits of memories: kids teasing, bullying. She didn't get along with other kids, she didn't fit in, she desperately wanted a friend.

Somehow, she knew this girl was a kindred spirit—precocious, opinionated, bright, and kindhearted. They would be fast friends.

"Yes. I want to be friends," she said, grinning now. "What's your name?"

"Kayla. What's yours?"

Susanna hesitated, suddenly nervous. What *was* her name? Who was she? Was she her mother again?

But then it came to her. "My name is Mary Grace."

It took Susanna a moment to realize she was in her grandmother's body this time.

"Ooh, you have two names. I love that." Kayla dug in the pocket of her skirt for a moment. "Here. I want you to have this. To say thank you. And for our friendship." Kayla handed her a folded piece of lined paper.

Susanna unfolded it. It was the same drawing of the bunny, only the paper wasn't yellowed. She smiled at Kayla.

"Now we're officially friends," Kayla said. "Can I teach you a game?"

Susanna nodded. Kayla started teaching her the game. It was sort of like patty-cake, but more complicated. Susanna giggled and just let herself enjoy it.

Suddenly, a shadow fell over them. "Young ladies, get back to the playground."

It was one of the teachers. She had a severe scowl on her face. As the girls stood, the teacher grabbed Mary Grace's arm. Kayla stopped.

"Go back to your part of the playground," the teacher said to Kayla. "Now move along."

Kayla hung her head and slowly walked off.

"Mary Grace, you know better than that."

"Better than what?" Susanna was surprised to hear her own thought, rather than Mary Grace's, vocalized.

The teacher tightened her grasp, digging her fingers into her arm. "You know you should not be playing with her kind."

Susanna froze and scanned the playground. White kids were on one side, and black kids were on the other.

Her shock overcame young Mary Grace's thoughts. "Are you serious? That's racist!"

Susanna didn't think it was possible, but the teacher dug her fingers and nails into her arm even tighter. She pulled her close and swung her other hand, swatting Mary Grace's behind sharply.

"I've had about enough of you, missy. Are you looking for detention? Would you like to visit the principal and his paddle?"

Susanna felt tears flowing from her eyes and heard herself sobbing. While her bottom—or rather, Mary Grace's bottom—stung, it was more the embarrassment and helplessness that drew forth the tears. Her emotions welled up and her surroundings swirled.

Then she felt herself falling backward.

Susanna had retreated to her room once again, even more confused and disoriented. She was still sitting on her bed, recalling the experiences over and over, when her mother and grandmother came into the house.

"Honey, we're home!"

Not wanting to be alone with her thoughts, she headed downstairs. Seeing her mother and grandmother immediately restored normalcy.

"Guess who won big?"

Nana held out a small stack of twenty-dollar bills. She tossed them straight up in the air and then spun around slowly, but with surprising grace, as they chaotically fluttered to the ground. Susanna was amused, but also slightly worried she might fall.

"What about the men, Nana?" Susanna asked teasingly.

With some surprise, she realized she had just called her Nana. It had just rolled off her tongue. It didn't sound as childish as it did when her mother said it.

"They couldn't stay away from me. That's because I'm beautiful—and now *rich*. Now I just have to decide which one will be my prince and which ones will get their hearts broken."

Margaret began picking up the twenties while Nana did a little jig.

"Oh yeah. It was quite the evening," Margaret said, giving Susanna a wide-eyed look. "But Nana needs to remember which of her suitors are still married. Those wives were not happy."

"Not my fault if their husbands fall for my charms," Nana said with a shrug. "Besides, at our age, there aren't many men left. They might just have to share."

Susanna giggled while her mom shook her head. Margaret put the collection of twenties on the kitchen counter, doing her best to straighten the stack. Then, yawning, she headed for the stairs.

"I tell you what," she said, looking at Susanna. "It wears me out, trying to keep up with your grandma. I'm headed to bed. Good night, ladies."

"Good night, dear," Nana said cheerfully.

When Margaret disappeared at the top of the stairs, Nana smiled at Susanna and put a finger to her lips. She found a small glass, then tiptoed to the high cabinet where Susanna's mom kept some liquor. Nana pulled out a bottle, poured herself a half glass, and then gestured for them to sit together at the kitchen island.

"Can you believe it, honey?" Nana asked. "Two hundred and fifty bucks, just like that!"

"That's great, Nana. But I want to talk to you about your memory box."

Nana raised her eyebrows and took a long sip from her glass. She drew in a sharp breath. "That's good whiskey." She set the glass down with a thud. "So, did you try the beads?"

Susanna nodded.

"And . . . ?"

Susanna dropped her voice to a whisper. "You're going to think I'm crazy, Nana, but I sort of . . . *fell* into your memories."

Her grandmother smiled and gently cupped Susanna's cheek. Susanna was surprised at the softness of her grandmother's hands.

"You're not crazy, Anna. That's how they work."

"But how? It can't be real. Did you hypnotize me? Am I hallucinating?"

Nana chuckled. "Little Anna. There's more to this world than science. There's more than just the things you see, touch, and feel. There's not much magic left in the world, and if some people had their way, it would all be gone. But if you open your mind, you can still find bits of it. Every time you see a rainbow, every time you watch the sunset, and every time you remember a dream—they're all little glimpses into what's beyond our world. The past and future. They're still out there—we're just passing through them. That's the secret to my painting. With the right charms, you can see the past and future, even if it's only a glimpse."

Susanna took a deep breath. "It felt so real, Nana. It felt like it was me, but I was Mom. I was painting a smiley face on a rock. You were painting too—one of the pictures you have in your room. I saw through Mom's eyes. I was little. And I smelled the paint."

Nana stroked Susanna's cheek again, then gently pushed her hair back from her face. "Oh honey, that's my favorite. My very favorite one. It's your mother's stone, your mother's memory."

"And then I was you. I met a little girl on the playground at your school. Her name was Kayla. You didn't have many friends, and she was so nice. She gave you a drawing of a bunny. That racist teacher didn't want you to play with her, but you must have. You must have become friends."

Nana sipped her whiskey. She pursed her lips and looked away, eyes staring off into nothing. She shook her head for a moment, then changed it to a nod.

"Yes, the best kind of friends—secret friends. Kayla taught me how to draw. She had such a passion for drawing. A natural talent. She unlocked something inside of me. We snuck off together every chance we had. We always got in so much trouble. You have to understand, though, honey—the black and white kids weren't supposed to play together back then."

"Oh, that's right," Susanna said. "We learned about segregation in school. But actually being there was . . . different."

Nana nodded, but she didn't seem to be listening to Susanna very closely. She smiled slightly as she reminisced. "Kayla made me want to become an artist. But later that year she moved away, and I never had any other close friends in elementary school. I was always getting in trouble. I was different. It's not easy to be different in school."

Susanna furrowed her brow, realizing for the first time that her grandmother had saved the drawing on purpose as a memento, even though it carried the hurt of losing a friend.

"But Nana, that's so sad. Why would you save that memory? Why would you want to relive that?"

"Not all the best memories are happy memories. Sometimes when you learn about the world, it's through pain and loss. I didn't want to forget what Kayla meant to me—as well as what she went through every day. What she still goes through, if she's as old as I am."

Nana sighed and took another sip of whiskey, then set the glass down and looked Susanna in the eyes.

"It's important to remember the things that make you who you are. On that day I met Kayla, I decided that no matter what, the teachers and other kids weren't going to change me. I decided it was OK for me to be different. I didn't have to think the way everyone else thought. Do you understand?"

"But Nana—" Susanna shook her head as if to object, but she unconsciously yawned instead.

Nana lifted her finger to her lips again. "Shhh. No more tonight. You're tired. I'm glad you were brave and opened your mind. But now, off to bed. You need your sleep. I promise it won't seem so strange and scary tomorrow."

Susanna began to speak again, but Nana firmly shook her head and pointed up the stairs. Still curious, but exhausted, Susanna reluctantly went up the stairs to her bedroom.

Susanna stood in Nana's doorway. Nana and her mom had gone off for a day of shopping. It had been a few days since she'd last been in the room—she'd forced herself to stay away, still torn between curiosity and fear.

The more time passed, the more she tried to tell herself it had all been a dream or a false memory. Part of her knew it had actually happened, but another part of her didn't want to admit it could be true. She wanted the universe to be guided by strict rules and hard lines. She didn't want it to be a flimsy cosmos, where you could simply slip inside someone else's memories just by holding some "magic beads." Yet she was still drawn to the box—drawn to the memories—every time she passed Nana's room.

Somehow she found herself sitting on the bed with Nana's memory box on her lap. She opened it and examined the contents without touching them. Her eyes went first to the yellow painted stone and then the yellowed note. Crystal-clear visions of the memories played in her mind. She smelled the paint and heard Kayla's voice in her head.

It was real. Or as real as it can be. Something happened.

Susanna examined the other items. As her hand reached out, her stomach dropped. She felt a mixture of dread and excitement. She paused, then picked up the paintbrush. Paint was still encrusted in the brush and streaked down the shaft. She drew in a breath and grasped the beads.

She fell once again.

She was standing in a room filled with easels. Tubes of paint were lined up on the easel tray in front of her. A window looked out to hedges and a grass football field beyond. There was no one else in the room, but she could hear the muffled sounds of people—other students—from the hallway and other classrooms.

She looked at the canvas in front of her. On it was a pencil sketch of a dancer leaping into the air in a grand jeté. It was only the frame of the dancer—lines for her limbs and circles for her joints. Her face was a blank oval. The rest of the painting was blank other than a line where the floor met the wall and a ballet barre running across the room.

A feeling of desire filled Susanna—Mary Grace's craving. A desire to create, a craving to flesh out the pencil sketch with form and shape and color. In her mind, she envisioned the silhouette, layers, and shades of the dancer. She pictured sharp lights from the ceiling and deduced bright spots and shadows.

Her mind saw rippling muscles and hair tight in a bun. She saw a reflection of the dancer in a mirror that did not yet exist. A tingle ran through her body. For the first time, Susanna allowed herself to take in the wonder of being in another time, another place, and another mind.

She picked up a paint palette and began squirting paint onto it: white, yellow, brown, and a dab of red. She chose a brush and mixed the colors, adding more brown paint bit by bit until she found the flesh tone she wanted. Without hesitation, she began making long brush strokes—a thick one for the torso, a slimmer one for a thigh, a delicate curve for a calf. She brushed in pointed feet without detail. She would layer white ballet slippers on top later.

She paused, breathless, as she viewed what she had created. When she finally took a breath, the familiar smell of paint filled her nostrils. Already, a recognizable body in motion, with good edges, filled the canvas.

The naked torso and blank face called out for color and detail. It would be treacherous to layer on muscle tone, lighting, and shadows on the skin without waiting for the first layer to dry. She knew she should move on to the barre behind the dancer or a light on the ceiling. Finding no patience, however, she succumbed to her need to realize the vision in her head.

She separated her flesh-tone paint into three sections. In one she added white; in another, black; and in the third, pink. Susanna was amazed at the subtle variations of color this created. She began with the pink hue, fleshing out muscle tone on first the dancer and then her reflection.

Pausing only to rinse the brush in a small can of water, she added the brighter highlights where the light struck the skin, then followed behind with the darker shadows. The wet paint blended beautifully under her confident strokes.

She stepped back once more, absorbing the results. Adrenaline poured through her veins as she saw her imagination come alive on the canvas. Again, she wished to add the hair, the eyes, and other bright colors that would add intensity and richness to the work. But there could be no skipping ahead this time, or the painting would be ruined. She would have to wait until the first layer dried. Susanna found herself caught up in the rush right along with Mary Grace.

Suddenly, she heard a voice behind her. She was so absorbed in the painting that it took a moment to register the words.

"Wow, that's sexy. I didn't know you drew nudes."

Mary Grace spun around and saw a blond boy leering at the painting. She turned back to the painting and immediately understood what he saw. She felt ashamed by the level of detail she had shown on the torso. It was unnecessary since it would eventually be covered by a simple red tutu, but all of the details had just flowed out of her. Her cheeks grew warm and her stomach flipped.

"It's not a nude," she said, talking quickly. "I have to wait for the paint to dry before I can layer on the clothing."

"Can you paint me one?" he asked with a smirk. "Let's see . . . a French girl lying on a chaise lounge with a feathered boa wrapped around her—but not covering too much?"

The boy was still staring at the painting, and Susanna felt Mary Grace's embarrassment grow. She struggled for a name, and eventually it came to her—Jeff. He was a rich kid, and one of the most popular kids in the school. Everyone she knew thought he was so handsome, so charming.

Mary Grace wasn't sure what to do. Since elementary school, she had been on the social outskirts, but she was finally making friends now in high school. She had to be careful. The wrong interaction with Jeff wouldn't just be embarrassing—it could outcast her completely. Susanna was surprised at just how much this worried Mary Grace. Nana never seemed to care what other people thought.

She decided to remain quiet. Her eyes down, she dropped her paintbrush into the can of water.

Jeff finally tore away his attention from the painting and focused on Mary Grace. "I'm serious. I want a sexy painting like this. I'll pay."

Mary Grace wanted to run. She barely spoke with boys, much less discussed nude paintings with them. She took a deep breath. "No. I told you—I don't paint nudes."

He smiled mischievously. It made Mary Grace guess that he didn't hear no often; it amused him. He looked her up and down with no attempt to disguise his stare. Her embarrassment turned to disgust.

"It's Mary Grace, right? I always thought you were weird, but you've really . . . How do I say this?" His smile grew. "You've really matured. What do you say you and I go out some night?"

Jeff took a step toward Mary Grace. She immediately took a step backward and nearly fell over the easel.

"No, thanks," she managed to say.

Jeff looked surprised for a moment, but he kept his smile. "What? I promise you we'd have a good time."

"Please leave me alone," she stuttered.

Jeff's smile turned to a scowl. Mary Grace became aware of how quiet the school had become.

"Jesus. What's your problem? What are you, a lesbian?"

She wasn't going to dignify his question with an answer. But her silence seemed to make a lightbulb go off in his head. His scowl returned to a smirk.

"You are!" he said. "That's why you paint naked girls."

Mary Grace began to walk around him toward the door. "Just leave me alone," she said again.

Jeff stepped in front of her, blocking her exit. He grabbed her shoulders, his fingers digging in. She stood stunned for only a moment before fear overtook her.

She twisted out of his arms and backed up. In a flash, she grabbed the only thing near her—the can of water. Without a moment's hesitation, she threw it at him. The can struck him in the face, the water spattered across his face, and the paintbrush struck his shirt. Susanna was surprised—Mary Grace hadn't so much as thought about the action beforehand.

As the can bounced noisily across the classroom floor, Jeff ran his hands down his face, wiping away as much water and paint as he could. He looked down at his shirt and then up at Mary Grace. His angry face was punctuated with browns, yellows, and reds.

She took a step backward. "I'm sorry," she said.

Immediately, the words tasted sour in her mouth. She looked over at her painting and was struck with the feminine grace and strength of the dancer. She turned back to Jeff, colors still running down his face and shirt, even discoloring his hair. She heard herself laugh and felt her fear dissolve.

She chose social outcast. Susanna cheered silently in the background.

"I take that back. I'm *not* sorry. My painting is *not* a nude—it's in progress. And I'm *not* ashamed of it. Even if it were a nude, I wouldn't be ashamed of it. And by the way: don't you ever put a hand on a girl without her permission, no matter who you are." She balled her fists and put on her most determined face.

Jeff looked confused.

Behind him, someone rushed into the room. "Is everyone OK?"

Jeff turned and looked at the boy, then quickly turned back to Mary Grace.

"You're crazy," he spat, pointing a finger at her. "I'm going to make sure every single person in this school knows what you are."

Jeff turned and stomped toward the door, kicking the can along the way. He drove his shoulder into the boy at the door, knocking the boy backward slightly.

The boy watched Jeff walk away, then met Mary Grace's eyes. "What was that all about?" he asked with concern, walking over to her.

Mary Grace was still trying to get her emotions under control. She looked at the dark-haired Latino boy. He was in her trigonometry class—a boy named Lucas. Mary Grace's hands relaxed as she managed a response. "Nothing. He put his hands on my shoulders, so I threw a can of water at him."

Lucas laughed. His smile lit up his face. "You threw a can of water at Jeff's face? Oh, I love it." He turned to the painting then, and his face went blank. "Wow," he murmured.

Mary Grace sighed. *Here we go again*, she thought. She was formulating her explanation when Lucas spoke again.

"You have so much talent," he said. "The motion, the reflection—I can't wait to see it when it's complete."

She searched his face. There was no leer, no smirk. Just wonder. She noticed his deep brown eyes and strong jaw, and her heart sped up a little.

"Thanks," was all she was able to get out.

She bent down to pick up the paintbrush. Just as she straightened up, he turned to face her, and they locked eyes. It took her breath away. She gripped the brush. She felt dizzy.

Then Susanna fell through.

Susanna sat up on the bed and dropped the beads. She felt a little weak. She took a deep breath to clear her head.

That memory had been a roller coaster—the thrill of painting, the shame of Jeff's taunting, the terror of his advances, the satisfaction of standing up to him, and the magic of looking in Lucas's eyes.

Lucas. That name was so familiar. Who was he?

With new determination, Susanna sorted through the memory box again, looking for the dog tags. Indeed, they read MENDEZ, LUCAS, along with a social security number, O POS, and CATHOLIC. Blood type and religion, she finally guessed.

It had to be the same Lucas. She glanced at the beads and remembered the roller coaster of the last memory. Who knew what was waiting for her this time?

But her curiosity overcame her fear. She reached for the beads and felt herself fall once again.

This time, she was sitting on a couch watching a show on an old television set. At least Susanna *guessed* it was a TV. The device was big and square, but the screen was small, rounded, and blurry. Lucy Ricardo was baking bread on-screen. A warm breeze blew through the screen door.

Susanna looked around and studied her reflection in the mirror above the fireplace. She was Nana again. Judging by the reflection, Mary Grace was older than she had been in the last memory, but not by much—maybe nineteen or twenty years old?

Most notably, her stomach was swollen. Susanna felt the extra weight, the sore back. But she searched Mary Grace's thoughts, and none of the discomfort even seemed to cross her mind. Something else was preoccupying her, though Susanna struggled to determine exactly what it was.

"You want a snack, sweetie?"

A face appeared around the corner. Susanna recognized her great-grandmother from the picture on Nana's mirror.

"I'm OK, Mom. I'm not hungry."

Mary Grace's mother retreated to the kitchen. Susanna's eyes scanned a picture on the wall. It was a wedding portrait of Mary Grace and Lucas!

Susanna was stunned. Was Lucas her grandfather? After all, Mary Grace was pregnant, and Margaret was her only child. But her mother's maiden name wasn't Mendez.

Susanna stared at the portrait as if searching for answers. Mary Grace's dress was white, elaborate, with a long train. Lucas wore a simple black tuxedo.

Mary Grace's feelings bled through Susanna as she studied his face. She too felt sadness, anxiety, and longing. Susanna searched Mary Grace's thoughts for an explanation, and it didn't take long to find it.

After that fateful day in the art room, Mary Grace and Lucas had fallen in love, only to see Lucas drafted when he turned eighteen. They quickly married right before he was sent to Korea. They had just one beautiful night before he left with the promise of a real honeymoon once he returned.

There was a knock at the door.

"I'll get it," her mom offered from the kitchen.

"No, it's OK," Mary Grace called back. "I'll get it."

She hopped off the couch and went to the screen door. Two men in full military uniform stood on the stoop with grim faces.

Mary Grace's feelings came rushing forward again, this time stronger, impossible to ignore—unbearable.

This was the visit she had been fearing but somehow expecting. She had lived every day in fear of this. Watching the news at night, waiting for his letters, waiting for the nightmare to end. She heard herself scream and her mother rushing in from the kitchen, also instantly understanding the reason for the soldiers at the screen door.

Mary Grace's mother hugged her daughter, who was still wailing and beginning to collapse. Anguish, grief, and loss welled up, along with the anxiety of raising a child alone.

Susanna fell away.

Her hands shaking, she dropped the dog tags into the box. She lay on the bed facedown and let herself sob into Nana's pillow.

Sometime later, Susanna felt soft hands caress her cheek. She opened her eyes. Nana was sitting on the bed next to her. Susanna realized that she had cried herself to sleep.

Bolting up straight, she stared at Nana. "Never again, Nana. Never again." She shook her head, tears returning. "Why would you let me go through that box? How could you put me through that? I want nothing to do with those beads. I don't want to touch them or even see them ever again!"

Nana put an arm around her and gave her a gentle squeeze. "I'm sorry, dear. I'm sorry." Glancing at the box, she saw the paintbrush and dog tags on top, near the beads. "You picked some of the hardest memories this time. But sometimes life is hard. I want to show you all this—the good, the bad—before I'm gone."

Susanna cycled through an erratic series of emotions: confusion, disbelief, anger, and just raw grief. "Why in the world would you want to show me those things?" She swatted at her tears.

Nana sighed. "I hid a lot from your mother. I never told her about her father. I even legally changed our last name from Mendez to my maiden name." She shook her head. "I know now that was all a mistake. That's why I want *you* to know about my life."

She touched one hand to the shoebox and the other to Susanna's arm.

"I want you to know that some memories are good; some are sad. Life isn't always fair. Not everyone is good. But that's why we need to cherish what *is* good about this world. Good or bad, things happen for a reason. What's important is to make the journey of your life an adventure. *That's* what I want you to learn from my memories."

They sat in silence. Susanna glanced into the shoebox at the paintbrush. She was beginning to understand why Nana had saved it. It truly did represent the good and the bad of life.

Nana's eyes followed Susanna's. "Dealing with that creep Jeff was awful—I don't love that part of that memory. But I still love thinking about the other parts of that day. It was the first time painting really fell into place for me. And it was the day I started getting to know your grandfather."

Susanna remembered the way Mary Grace had painted, the feelings of joy, the desire to create, to bring her vision to life.

"I want to paint too, Nana," she suddenly said, surprising herself. "I want to feel that way."

Nana's eyes lit up. "Really, dear? I would love to teach you!"

They hugged, rocking each other back and forth.

"I'm glad you're living with us, Nana," Susanna said, pushing herself back to look Nana in the eyes. "I want to know more about your life. But from now on, can we do it the old-fashioned way? Can you just tell me stories?"

Nana chuckled. "Of course, Anna—I mean, Susanna," she corrected herself.

"Actually . . . it's OK," her granddaughter replied, smiling. "I think Anna is growing on me."

Nana gave her hand a tight squeeze. "You'll paint your own memories, Anna."

Anna squeezed Nana's hand back, then headed for her room, on a mission. She knew just what she needed.

A shoebox.

The End

I've always been intrigued by the possibility of terraforming a world. However, when I began to write about it, I realized it needed something else. So I added in a love story . . . sort of.

A QUESTION OF MOTIVATION

Love makes you stupid.

Liza appears on the interdisplay. As always, she looks flawless: yellow-blond hair pulled back in a bun accenting her high cheekbones, full red lips, blue eyes. She makes my heart stammer even after all this time.

"How's the growth in Biodome 2?" she asks.

"Incredible," I say, looking around. "This soil is perfect. I'll be bringing back a huge load of vegetables in the rover. And the rabbits had babies again. We'll need to harvest some of those soon."

"Bring one back," she says. "I'll make salad and rabbit stew for dinner. We'll celebrate."

"Celebrate what?" I ask.

"It's your two-year anniversary! Parker, you've been out of cryo for two years. And we should also celebrate how well the terraforming is progressing."

Sometimes, she has a way of making me feel a little inadequate with her remarkable memory and attention to detail. Has it really been two years?

My thoughts drift back even earlier, to the eight of us—six crew members and two alternates—training for nine months. The training was brutal, physically and mentally. But it drew us all together.

And we all immediately fell for Liza, even Franco and Bennie, the alternates. That's because Liza has a brightness about her. Everyone wanted to be around her, whether they sought friendship or something more. For those of us with romantic interests, though, acting on our feelings was out of the question. There was no time for a relationship, and she was our colleague, so we all kept the feelings to ourselves.

We finished the nine months without incident. Then the six of us said goodbye to Franco and Bennie, who were kicked back to the next mission. Our six-person crew boarded our brand-new ship, the *Condicio*; underwent cryopreservation; and began our mission.

A forty-two-year one-way trip to Veriff B.

Veriff B is a dry, rocky planet the corporation has been terraforming for hundreds of years. They'd been bombarding it with nearby icy asteroids, adding water and kicking dust into the atmosphere, causing global warming.

By the time we were to arrive, that phase would be completed. We would have been one of several ships to begin building habitats and seeding life. It would have been difficult work in a harsh environment—a planet that doesn't want to be terraformed.

However, there's already a terraformed planet in the system, Veriff A. So after about ten years of work on Veriff B, we were supposed to retire to a life of luxury on Veriff A. Ten years of backbreaking work in exchange for an early retirement on a beautiful planet rich in resources and low in population? Not a bad deal. It would sure beat rotting away on our polluted, overcrowded Earth.

That was what was supposed to happen. But about two-thirds of the way to our destination, we had an engine failure. Odds were one in a million, but it happened to us.

The computer woke Captain Cepper from his cryogenic slumber while the rest of us slept away. Cepper immediately sent a distress signal that wouldn't even be heard back at Earth for over seventy years.

Personally, I think he should have awoken a second crew member right away. In his defense, though, official mission protocol doesn't address main engine failure—it just isn't supposed to happen. And waking a crew member would have been a huge drain on resources.

But anyway, after he woke up, Cap did something amazing: somehow, he found a nearby planet. Stumbling upon a planet like this one was as improbable as the engine's failure. People have been hunting for habitable planets for hundreds of years. They are as rare as a single grain in a bucket of sand.

He would later name the planet Bethia. My guess is that it's a nod to Liza's full name, which most people don't know. The planet has four moons, all small and none habitable.

Unlike Veriff B, this planet turned out to be perfect for terraforming: rocky, an existing atmosphere, a strong magnetic field, and plenty of water. It's almost too perfect . . . which makes me wonder: How did we randomly fall out of hyperspace and manage to be just in reach of an ideal planet? And if this planet is along the route between Earth and the Veriff System, why hadn't it been discovered before?

Cepper put us in orbit and used the dropship to descend to the planet. He built the habitat and assembled two oxygen generators without bringing anyone out of cryo. The structures are designed to be a single person job for emergencies, but it's back-breaking work in an uncomfortable suit. I suppose he wanted to make sure there was plenty of oxygen before waking anyone.

Apparently, he worked alone for nearly a year before he sustained a life-threatening injury in a rover accident. He returned to the ship just in time to wake Liza—and die.

How'd you build the entire habitat on your own yet then die by rolling the rover, Cap? Why didn't you wake one of us earlier to help?

After Cap's death, Liza woke Markus to help her build the first biodome—only to have him die as well. Shortly after they finished the biodome, his suit failed, and less than ten minutes later, he died of asphyxiation.

Did I mention that terraforming is dangerous business?

Liza woke me next. Together, we built another biodome. Darlene and Tyrell are still in cryo, orbiting above us.

That's the short version, anyway. A lot more happened in between all this, and even I don't know all the details. I've been out of cyro for two years, and plenty of things still don't make sense to me.

These missing details and nagging questions have been plaguing me for a few days now. It all started when I had my own little suit glitch. Luckily, I was right outside Biodome 2 when it happened. It wasn't even a close enough call to set off the emergency warnings.

"Parker, hon?" Liza calls out, breaking me from my trance. "You OK? Are you finished there?"

"Oh, yeah. Sorry. Just daydreaming." I let out a breath and shake my head. "I just need to pack up the rover. I'll be there in fifteen minutes."

Despite the heat and humidity, I love being in the biodomes. No suit. So green—nothing like the desert browns of the rest of the planet. And all this *space*. The domes are fifty meters in diameter, which seem huge when you spend all your time in cramped spaceships and habitats.

I've spent this whole morning in Biodome 2, trimming plants, restocking the rabbit auto-feeders, and just puttering around. It's given me lots of time alone to think about the improbable fate that brought us here, Cap, Markus . . .

Liza.

Liza pulls the rabbit out of the basket I brought her. The rabbit struggles in her hands at first but goes limp when she strokes its fur and whispers to it. Then, in one quick motion, she snaps its neck.

Jesus. Pioneer woman, I guess. But when I first met her back in training, I never would have imagined.

"Babe, would you mind getting a bottle of red from the back storage?" she asks sweetly. "One of the good ones. Remember, we're celebrating." She gives me a peck on the cheek and a grin before turning her attention back to the rabbit.

I trudge off down the back hallway to the storage compartment and hunt around for the good wine. I'm about to give up, but then I find it way in back, behind a box of emergency rations. When I return to the kitchen, Liza is ripping the skin and fur from the rabbit. She's humming, but a pot of boiling broth keeps me from deciphering the tune.

"The drones are making good progress," she says as she works. "The cyanobacteria spraying in the northern cliffs is finished, and they're about fifty percent done with the algae seeding in the southern lake. The drones brought back some water samples. The results look promising."

"That's fantastic," I say.

"We'll need to take a trip out to the cliffs. I've been studying the photos from the drones, but they kick up a lot of dust. It's hard to see how the cyanobacteria are doing."

"That's a long trip in the rover."

Liza starts cutting the rabbit up into parts. She's good with a knife. "We might be able to use the dropship," she suggests. "I'll check the charts to see if the terrain is flat enough for a landing. If not, we'll just bring an overnight emergency tent and a power gen. It'll be like camping out. Might even be romantic." She smiles and gives me a wink.

I try to smile back, but I don't want to spend a night in a flimsy emergency tent—and I can't seem to tear my eyes away from the blood on her hands.

"Hopefully there's a good spot for the dropship," I say. "That'll make things a lot easier."

I begin tearing up a head of lettuce while Liza washes the blood from her hands. She picks up the knife and begins chopping the root vegetables I brought.

I don't even know why, but my mind instantly goes back to those same gnawing questions. What were the odds of Cap and Markus both having fatal accidents? Yes, working in an unfriendly atmosphere is dangerous. But these guys were pros. And each one died shortly after completing a major task on the planet.

These thoughts move from my brain to my mouth without getting filtered along the way. "Liza, did Cap tell you anything before he died? Did he say why he waited so long before he woke anyone?"

She's deftly slicing through the carrots and potatoes but pauses briefly at my question. "Where's this coming from?" she asks.

"I don't know," I say. "Feeling nostalgic with my two-year anniversary, I guess."

She resumes her chopping, cutting so quickly that I worry about her fingers. She seems irritated.

"I was so groggy. I barely remember. He could hardly speak. He'd already lost a lot of blood. He just told me that the habitat was ready. I was still in the cryochamber. He touched my cheek and then collapsed. By the time I got out of the chamber, he was dead."

She dumps the vegetables and the rabbit meat into the boiling broth in one swift motion.

"Why did you bury him before waking Markus? It must've been tough to move his body and dig the grave in your suit."

Liza looks me squarely in the eyes as she dries her hands on a towel. I know she's wondering where I'm going with this conversation.

"It *was* very hard. In more ways than one. But it was just something I felt I had to do." She sets the towel aside and takes a deep breath, letting it out in a sigh. "Do we have to discuss this tonight? We're supposed to be celebrating."

"Sorry. I've been thinking about how long it's been since we were in cryo and how well the terraforming is going . . . I guess it all got me thinking about Cap. I still can't believe he found this planet. And that he got the hab built all on his own."

Liza searches in a drawer, then hands me an old-fashioned corkscrew. "Yeah. We owe him a lot." She lets a small smile slip through her serious demeanor. "Now, will you please open the wine and pour us each a glass? The stew won't take long."

We have a fantastic dinner and lose ourselves in talk about everything but the accidents. Liza's smile and the wine allow me to temporarily put aside my concerns. When the bottle is empty and we're ready for more than conversation, Liza passionately reminds me why I've fallen so deeply in love with her.

After looking at the charts, we confirm we'll have enough even terrain to land the dropship near the cliffs. But that doesn't exactly ease my concerns. The one patch of even terrain is on the top of the cliffs . . . which are over three thousand meters tall.

You see, I'm a bit scared of heights. I typically don't have an issue with flying in an atmosphere. But put me on a tall building or ledge, and my breathing gets rapid, my palms get sweaty, and I start feeling dizzy.

Some spaceman, huh?

Liza and I sit at the controls in the dropship, waiting for the gravity coils to warm before takeoff. In these moments where I'm just killing time, my thoughts keep returning to the same old topic. I don't know why. I can't put my finger on it exactly. All I know is that I need to fill in these gaps.

"So, now that we're not 'celebrating' anymore, do you mind if I ask . . . how long after Cap died did you wake Markus?"

She slowly closes and then reopens her eyes, clearly frustrated. "I don't know. A couple days, I guess. We needed to get the biodome built, and I didn't want to do it alone. Markus was primary on biodome construction, so I woke him."

She pulls up the preflight on her display and begins reviewing it. But I know she has it memorized. It's not going to stop my questions.

"And the two of you spent a whole year constructing the biodome and planting the gardens. Don't you think it would have gone faster if you had woken another of us up?"

She doesn't turn away from the display. "Another person wouldn't have made it go any faster. Everything was designed to be constructed with minimal labor that two people can handle as easily as three. You saw it when we put together Biodome 2. Besides, we didn't want to jeopardize the oxygen or food supplies. Remember, we weren't sure the biodomes would be so successful. Having three or four of us on line would have reduced the reserves quickly. If the biodome wasn't successful, we would've been in trouble."

I pause and think back to when I—when we all—first met Liza. She was so beautiful and sweet. All I could think about was her, but I never acted on my feelings during those nine months of training, and I never knew whether she felt the same way about me.

But once she brought me out of cryo, it didn't take long to find out. It was just the two of us. A couple of weeks, and we were lovers.

Was it any different for Markus? I'm afraid of the answer, but I ask anyway.

"And the two of you . . . you never developed feelings for each other after a year of being alone together?"

She flips the display back to the gravity coils status. It takes her a few moments to speak.

"He made a few initial attempts to flirt—maybe just to gauge my interest. But once I made it clear we would only be friends, he was nothing but professional."

I try to study Liza's eyes, to see if she's blinking or looking away, to get a revealing glimpse of what she really felt for Markus. But she's still fixated on her display.

"Must have been rough on the guy, working beside you for a year," I say, intentionally stirring her up, hoping to get a little deeper. "I mean, he was literally the only man on the planet, and you wanted to be 'just friends.'"

She turns and glares at me now. "Yes, Parker. Obviously, it was rough on him. But it wasn't exactly easy on me, either."

"Sorry. You're right," I say sincerely.

She turns back to the display, but her eyes don't seem to focus on it. "I think he did fall for me," she says softly. "But he just wasn't my type. We managed, but it could get awkward at times. He used to take long walks just to blow off steam. That's why he was out there when his suit failed."

This is new information for me. I sit forward, my heart rate increasing. "You mean he was just out for a *stroll* when his suit failed?" My voice comes out higher than usual. "I thought it happened while he was working construction on the biodome. If he was just out for a walk, why couldn't he make it back in time?"

"He was five kilometers out. I always asked him not to go so far, but he ignored me. As soon as the emergency warnings went off, I suited up and ran a rover out to him . . . but he was dead by the time I reached him." Her voice is emotionless. I think she'd like to be done digging up the past.

We hear a satisfying chime signifying that the coils are sufficiently heated.

"And you buried him before you woke me . . ."

I know this part of the story—I visited his and Cap's graves not long after I was stable. But still, I need to hear it from her. Again.

"Yeah," she replies flatly. "It was a lot like with Cap. It wasn't easy, but I felt like it was something I needed to do before moving on. Besides, the last thing you would have wanted to do just as you came out of cryo was dig a grave."

"I guess you're right," I mumble.

She flicks a couple of switches overhead. "Okay, she's ready. Shall we head to the cliffs?"

I take a deep breath. "Yeah. I'm as ready as I'll ever be."

Liza is silent during the flight. It's a clear signal for me to keep my mouth shut too.

I take the opportunity to try to silence my mind as well. These questions have to stop. They're driving Liza crazy—and me too. I have to accept that some questions can't be answered. Some mysteries can't be solved.

For instance, there's no way to explain why or how we ended up here on this planet.

Just wait until the corporation hears about this, decades from now. Only two things matter to the corporation: costs and profits. They're all about terraforming planet systems as cost-effectively as possible. They'll be pleased to hear that instead of toiling away and blowing budgets on Veriff B, our little crew stumbled upon an undiscovered planet ripe for terraforming.

In fact, I bet the corporation will be *very* pleased . . .

The gnawing returns. I turn and gaze out at the massive cliff wall ahead. Liza accelerates and begins to ascend while my stomach drops. Had the whole mission been to terraform this planet, not Veriff B, all along? Would the corporation expect us to carry out an unplanned mission with no hope of a rescue? What if, in our despair, we hadn't even bothered with seeding this world?

Yet we did—we did start the terraforming. Or better yet, *she* did. Cap built the hab, yes. But since then, Liza has been the driving force behind the terraforming, with help first from Markus and now from me.

Now I find myself turning my head toward her. I study her, how perfect she is: perfect skin, perfect smile, perfect health. In the two years we've been together, she's never so much as complained of a headache . . .

A strange thought suddenly flutters into my consciousness. Back on Earth, just before we'd left, there had been rumors of a new type of android-clone hybrid. They're completely biologically engineered, are capable of superhuman strength, have a life span of several hundred years.

The fluttering stops, but the thought remains.

Could it be possible? Could Liza be one of those hybrids? And if so, could it be possible that even she doesn't realize it? Has Liza been programmed to use the rest of us one by one to successfully complete this mission?

How did Cap and Markus *actually* die?

I'm numb. I force myself to move my fingers and toes, trying to clear out this paralyzing effect. Am I just paranoid? I mean, Liza is my *lover*. But more than that, she's my best friend. She makes me laugh, makes me happy. How could she be anything but human?

Then again, maybe becoming lovers was all part of the plan. As we were building the second biodome, I was falling in love. It made the work go fast. It kept me distracted. And it also meant I wasn't asking many questions.

"What are you thinking about, hon?" she asks, startling me slightly. "You're white as a ghost."

"Oh, I'm just nervous about the cliffs," I improvise.

Her perfect face softens. "Well, don't worry. If you like, I can do the rappelling. You can just hold things down at the top. How's that?"

"That makes me feel better." I nod. "Thanks, babe."

The display beeps, and Liza returns her attention to the controls. "OK, here's our spot. Prepare for landing."

Liza puts the dropship down about two hundred meters from the cliff wall. It means some walking, but we don't want any chance of the cliff wall collapsing under the weight of the dropship. We put on our helmets and unload the gear into a pull cart with big knobby tires. Thank God we have that little cart, because the winch we need weighs a ton.

Walking in a suit is always cumbersome, but I feel particularly uneasy right now. This insane idea about Liza is weighing me down.

"Liza, can I ask you something?" I ask, unable to help myself.

She gives me a stern look. "Maybe. Is it about the past? Because right now, we're supposed to be building something for our future."

"No, it's not about the past," I say truthfully. "It's just— why are you so focused on taking the terraforming this far? Like, I know the biodomes are important for our survival, but the algae and these cyanobacteria won't make a difference until long after we're dead."

The cart moves effortlessly as we pull it along the flat ground.

"Well, it's our mission," she says simply. "We're here, and we have the technology and the supplies. Don't you want to help humanity spread across the stars? Isn't that why you signed up for this?"

I let out a slight laugh. "I signed up because I had a crappy job, a crappy apartment, and a crappy life on Earth. I signed up because I could retire rich after ten years."

"Well, aren't you altruistic," Liza says, sounding exasperated.

"What I'm saying is, *that* was the mission. But then the engine failed, and the mission was over."

The cart hits a bump, but the large tires absorb it. We're about halfway to the cliffs.

"I just want to make the best of our situation," she says. "We can create a habitable world here. It won't be completed in our lifetime, but we can give life a foothold on this planet. It's more than most people accomplish in their lives." She laughs a bit. "What do you suggest we do instead? Sit in the hab and play cards all day?"

"No, but we could focus on building Biodome 3. Then we might be in a better position to wake Darlene and Tyrell. We haven't even talked about when to wake them."

She stops the cart and turns toward me. "You picked a strange time to discuss this, Parker. What is this all about?"

"I guess . . . I don't know." I kick at the dirt a little, head down. All my crazy thoughts and questions seem so ridiculous now. "Maybe I'm just kind of depressed. This whole anniversary thing got me thinking about being on this planet for the rest of my life."

"Are you getting tired of me or something?"

The question stuns me. I can't see her face because of the sun glinting off her visor.

"No, not at all," I reply quickly. "Honestly, if it weren't for you, I probably would have walked out an air lock without my helmet by now."

"Don't say that," Liza says softly, taking a step toward me. "We're building a world here. And more importantly, we have each other. I thought that meant something to you. Don't you want to make a life with me?"

I still can't make out her facial expression, but I see her head tilt slightly.

"No. I mean, yes. I love you, Liza." I try to catch my breath and thoughts. "It's just . . . I could handle living in cramped habs and space suits knowing there was a big green planet with a clean atmosphere waiting for me ten years down the line. I guess the realization that I'll never walk suit-less under a blue sky again is just sinking in."

"How about this?" she says, putting a reassuring hand on my shoulder. "We'll continue to expand the terraforming, but we'll also build Biodome 3 together, just like you suggested. With three biodomes, we'll have all the food and air we need. Then we can even add on to the hab. We have time. We've got the 3-D printers and plenty of raw materials. Maybe we'll wake Darlene and Tyrell at the end of our lives so they can continue the terraforming after we're gone. They might live long enough to start planting the more complex flora."

Or maybe you'll kill me after I help with a few more tasks, and then you'll wake them one at a time to give you the maximum help for terraforming with minimal resources. But I shake that fear out of my head almost as quickly as it had popped in there.

"You're right," I say. "That would be great for Darlene and Tyrell. I mean, how many people get a chance to be Adam and Eve?"

Liza begins to pull the cart again, and I follow her lead.

"I know what you're feeling," she says as we walk. "But I just hope you mean it when you say you love me. Sometimes, I worry." She sighs. "Anyway, we need to get moving. We can talk more about this later."

We pull in silence until we reach the cliff edge. Liza unloads the gear, and I take a moment to check out the horizon spanning in front of us—it's a deliberate attempt to look out, not down.

Thankfully, the view is majestic. From our vantage point, we can see two large lakes and a winding river. There are small foothills below us and off to the west, but most of the land is flat plains. I try to spot our biodomes but can't locate them. I'm not sure if they're beyond the horizon or just too small to make out.

Then I take a step forward and try to look down the cliff face. It's a dizzying distance, and my heart immediately starts pounding.

Without warning, something pushes me from behind. I let out a high-pitched shriek.

In a split second, my mind flashes back to my first training space walk. We were at the corporation's primary space station. They called it the Doorstep. When we floated out the hatch, I immediately became disoriented. They'd warned us not to focus on Earth, which loomed below, but to keep our eyes on the station. Well, I failed miserably. I looked directly down at Earth, and the sensation of falling hit me. The instructor had to grab me and talk me out of my panic. It was humiliating, and it almost washed me out.

By the time that second passes, I realize Liza is behind me, having given me a playful shove but still holding firmly onto me.

"Shit—I'm sorry, baby," she says, sincerely remorseful yet trying to hide her laughter. "I know you're afraid of heights. I was just teasing. I shouldn't have done that."

I try to use logic to calm myself. If my fears about her were true, she would have pushed me over the edge. Right? But then again, maybe she's just toying with me, putting me in my place after all these pushy questions.

I'm driving myself crazy with doubts.

"Christ, Liza," I finally say. "It's a good thing this suit has a catheter—you scared the piss out of me. Give me a second to catch my breath."

She laughs outright now.

I still feel nervous being so close to the edge with her directly behind me. I break free of her and walk back to the pull cart. With every step, I feel my heart rate drop and my breathing slow.

"I'm sorry, but you squealed like a little girl." She's still laughing. "I'll make it up to you later. I promise."

Her reference to "later" calms my nerves a little. "You better. Now, how the hell does this winch work?"

We work together to set up the heavy winch that will lower Liza down the cliff edge. I hammer in the spikes that anchor it in place. The rope is lightweight but strong. From my perspective, though, it looks too thin to hold a person.

"You sure this line is safe?" I ask. "It's so thin."

"It's rated to over five hundred kilograms. Don't worry."

I try not to worry, but it still makes me nervous. I'm ashamed to admit it to myself, but I'm glad it will be Liza climbing down.

"Did you get the spikes solidly into the rock?" she asks as she clips in.

I take a deep breath. "Yes. Everything's harder with the suit on, but they went in easily."

"OK! Down I go!"

Without hesitation, she swings out to the cliffside, planting both her feet onto the cliff wall. She gives me a smile and a wink.

"OK, you can start lowering me. I'll look for signs of the bacteria. They'll be subtle, just patches of red or orange, so go slow."

I begin lowering her down. After about fifteen meters, I hear her voice over the suit com.

"Nothing yet. This cliff wall is pure rock—just what the bacteria are engineered for. I'm just worried it hasn't been able to get a foothold."

I let the winch run, my finger just over the Halt button.

"Stop!" she cries.

Panicked, I hit the button, and the winch pauses. My heart jumps.

"Are you OK? Liza?" I call out.

I try to look over the cliff, but my body won't let me get close enough to the edge.

Still silence. It has only been seconds, but it feels like forever.

"Liza? Are you there? Is everything OK?"

"Yeah, everything's fine," she finally replies. "I think I found a patch. I'm about twenty-five meters down. I'm taking some pictures and some samples. Give me about five or ten minutes."

Relieved, I take a step back from the edge. I check the anchors in the stone, and they seem to be staying put. The line is tight, and everything looks good.

Then I look at the line again. I have a utility knife in a pocket on my suit. It's standard issue.

I find myself wondering if it's sharp enough to cut the line.

One by one, the emotions I've felt over the last two years start passing through my mind—or maybe my body. The confusion when waking from cryo. The concern about the damaged ship. The grief over Cap and Markus. The attraction to Liza overcoming all else. I remember going planetside and exploring the hab and the biodome, falling in love, dropship runs to the *Condicio* for materials and supplies, making love to Liza in free fall, building the second biodome. In so many ways, the two years have gone by fast.

"Parker, this is excellent. The bacteria are healthy and spreading."

"That's wonderful," I reply, trying my best to keep my voice steady.

I pull my utility knife out of its pocket, uncap it, and stare at the blade as it glints in the sun. I picture Liza falling, plummeting over three thousand meters to the ground. I wonder what she would think, knowing it was me who cut the line. I picture her broken and lifeless at the base of the cliff. I think about life without her.

That very thought wrings my heart.

I love her. Android, clone, or human—whatever she's done or not done, I don't care. I love her.

I put the cap on the knife and return it to my suit pocket. A wave of euphoria washes through me. It doesn't matter if she'd been born, cloned, or manufactured. It doesn't matter why she loves me. The fact is, she and I are alone on this planet. And we are in love.

I realize then that I want to terraform this planet too. So what if that was the corporation's plan all along, if we've been misled and lied to? I have no other options. I have to terraform this planet. What could anyone accomplish in a lifetime that was more important than bringing life to a dead world?

"I'm done," Liza says over the com. "Bring me up, Parker."

No turning back.

I press the button, and the winch begins spinning, slowly pulling her up the cliff. It's then that I notice the anchors have pulled up a little from the rock. I quickly step onto the base of the winch and hit the Halt button.

"Liza, put as much of your weight as you can onto the cliff wall," I say quickly and with more panic than I expect.

"Why? What's going on?" Her voice rises an octave.

"The anchor spikes are pulling out a little." I try to calm myself, not wanting to scare her. "I guess this rock is softer than I thought. It's OK. I'm standing on the base. It should help. I'm restarting the winch slowly. Try to walk up the cliff wall, keeping as much of your weight on the wall as possible." I restart the winch.

"It's not that easy," she replies, her voice tense. "I can't get that much weight on my feet. Is it holding?"

I bend to examine the spikes, careful not to lift any weight off them. It's all moot, of course—I'm aware that my weight likely can't stop the winch if the spikes give way.

Before I can respond, Liza speaks again. "Parker? I'm scared."

I feel little shocks through the rope. She must be hopping, pushing out to get her feet on the wall. With each shock, the anchors pull a little looser. I stop the winch again.

"OK, this isn't working," I say, my heart racing. "Forget using the cliff wall. Just hang and let the winch pull you up. When you get to the top, though, you'll have to pull yourself up. I can't take my weight off the winch."

I restart the winch. It's hard to tell, but the anchor spikes seem to be gradually lifting as she nears the edge. It'll be close. I feel sweat beading on my forehead.

"Liza, as soon as you get to the edge, grab on."

Now I can see the anchors are clearly pulling out of the rock. The entire winch tilts toward the cliff. It feels like the whole thing will go over any second.

The winch stops.

"I'm here." She sounds weary.

I see Liza's hands. She reaches for the cliff wall, but the winch arm keeps her a little bit away from the edge. She can brush the edge with her fingers, but she's not close enough to get a good grip. She claws at the rock.

"Parker!" she shrieks.

I feel it giving way. For a second, I realize this is my last chance to change my mind.

Just as the anchors pull completely from the ground, I dive at Liza, reaching out and just managing to grasp one wrist. A second later, I feel a tremendous jolt as the falling winch tries to pull Liza down.

She screams, but I hold on. Somehow, I hold on with a strength I have never found before. Then I brace myself and lift Liza, hefty winch and all. I rise to my knees and place her on the ground next to me.

That's when I realize what I am—what we both are.

I pull the winch up the rest of the way and unclip Liza. She stares at me, wide-eyed—maybe with distrust. Then something changes in her eyes, and she collapses into me, hugging me tightly.

"Oh God, Parker. You saved me."

evening sky.

we are here, and we have a world to terraform. We look out at our world—a virgin world to which we have brought life, a world where we will build a life together.

It is enough.

The End

Having raised a daughter and coached girls' soccer, I know all too well the surprising will and tenacity of young girls. It recently struck me how easily beings not of this planet might underestimate a pre-teen girl from Earth. In this tale, a random life-form is selected periodically to rule the galaxy. A twelve-year-old Earth girl named Sally Ann has been chosen and will soon be unleashed upon her unsuspecting subjects. She's going to make some changes . . .

SALLY ANN, QUEEN OF THE GALAXY

Sally Ann awoke abruptly, her pale blue eyes fluttering open. She lay still at first, noticing the copy of Lewis Carroll's novel still balanced on her chest from the night before. She moved the book to her nightstand, slid her elbows back, and lifted her shoulders and head. Her blond curls followed, bouncing to a stop. She scanned the bedroom.

Pink frilly curtains, pink walls, porcelain rabbits, and wooden horses. *I'm twelve, almost thirteen, and I still have the room of an eight-year-old girl. I would be embarrassed to bring a friend here. That is, if I had any friends. But friends or no friends, I need to grow up. I need to face my new responsibilities. Just like Alice, I give myself good advice but very seldom follow it.*

Sally Ann sat up in bed and crossed her legs—*crisscross applesauce*, she thought. She yawned and stretched, reaching first toward the ceiling and then out wide. She looked out the window, stretching forward to see between the parted pink ruffled curtains. Sunshine was pouring into the room.

She could just make out the swing as it swayed in the early morning breeze.

Her door opened, and Spot padded into the room, his floppy ears bouncing with every step, not unlike Sally Ann's blond curls.

"Spot! Oh, Spot. Good morning!"

He stopped at the base of her bed, making eye contact as his head tilted slightly to the side.

"Uppy, uppy. Come on. Hop up here, Spot."

Spot crouched and then leaped adeptly onto the bed, landing softly next to Sally Ann. She smiled and ruffled the white fur on his head and then lightly kissed the same spot.

"At least you're my friend, right, Spot?"

"Yes, I'm most definitely your friend, Miss Sally Ann. But you know my name is Alspotemis. I would prefer that you call me by my proper name."

Spot knew she wouldn't, but it was a morning ritual that had begun nearly five years ago. They both seemed to enjoy the routine.

"Oh, there's far too much *proper* around here," she said. "And a name shouldn't be required to prop oneself up." She paused and smiled, a glint in her eyes. "But if you return me to my home, I'll call you by any name you wish."

"Miss Sally Ann, you know you will be returned to your home on your eighteenth birthday—not a moment sooner and not a second later. It is beyond my control, and it saddens me to hear you ask."

She grabbed Spot gently by both ears and moved her face close to his. "It saddens me more to be denied." She sighed. "I wish to skip lessons and go for a walk in the gardens this morning."

Alspotemis struggled to back away, but Sally Ann had a firm grip on him. "You cannot skip lessons. It is forbidden."

Sally Ann released Spot and fell back onto the bed. "OK, then I want to rearrange the day's agenda. I would like to reschedule some exercise to an earlier slot—say, in fifteen minutes, after I dress. Oh, and please tell Gandemille that I want to redecorate my room."

Spot moved up on the bed, closer to Sally Ann, and sat. "I know what you're doing. You're trying to reschedule and extend activities until you run out of time for your lessons. You're not fooling anyone."

Sally Ann reached behind Spot's ear and scratched. "If you're denying my request for exercise, I'm happy to file a dispute request. It's form A23-7324B-3. And if you file an expedited resolution request, I'll file another dispute request citing my inalienable right to modify my corporeal isometrics activities based on my species' needs, for which you will be required to produce an unbiased *Homo sapiens* adept to testify. And if you manage to produce—"

With regret, Spot pulled away from Sally Ann's hand and attempted to look serious. "Please stop, Miss Sally Ann. May I point out that engaging in an all-day pseudolegal skirmish is in itself a lesson in galactic protocols and regulations? A highly inefficient lesson, but nevertheless, it—"

Sally Ann gently pushed Spot onto his back and began scratching his belly. She moved her hand around until she found the spot that made his leg twitch.

"Who wants to go for a walk? You do. Yes, you do. You want to go for a walk. Don't you, boy?"

"OK, OK, OK—we'll reschedule your lessons to this afternoon and schedule exercise this morning," he said, attempting and failing to sound authoritative. "But please, no more reschedules after this morning. If you truly believe in your principles, then the implications of implementing those principles are vast. There is much to do and little time to do it. You have great responsibilities."

"No responsibilities are great," Sally Ann said with a sigh.

What did Alice say? she thought to herself. *"It's no use going back to yesterday, because I was a different person then."*

She smiled again and continued rubbing her companion's furry belly. "Now, that's a good boy. Yes, that's a good Spot."

Spot, still on his back with his leg twitching, did his best to compose himself. "Miss, may I remind you that I am one hundred fifty-seven Earth years old? I am an elder statesman for my species, an official galactic representative, and serving as your personal advisor—a role that typically involves a formal, professional relationship."

Sally Ann's smile didn't falter for a moment. "Yes, and you're a good boy who's going to go on a walk! Yes, you are."

Spot groaned, but he didn't stop Sally Ann from scratching the right spot on his belly.

"Dake, are you telling me I should be worried?" Consul Casifel asked, marching hastily into the intelligence center, his pace quite opposite his typical measured, confident gait. His red cloak billowed behind him and then settled quickly as he stopped. His nearly translucent white skin contrasted sharply with his formal red uniform.

"I'm apathetic concerning your emotional state," Dake replied as he walked languidly in the consul's wake, his purple face blank. "I'm merely conveying the facts." He noticed with satisfaction that Casifel was gritting his rather large teeth, causing tendons to ripple in his neck.

"Well, regardless, I'm worried. I need to know how worried I should be. What's her current galactic approval rating?"

Dake's eyes trembled upward inside his head, accessing the tech-link embedded there. His species' gelatinous purple skin was more tolerant of implanted technology than most.

"Eighty-nine percent. She is apparently 'adorable,' 'delightful,' 'charming,' and 'refreshing.' At least, that's how most planets and species are reporting. Your decision long ago to record and broadcast the leader designate's every waking minute seems to have had an unintended effect in this case."

Casifel stepped up to a data pedestal and invoked a hologram with a complex hand motion. He waved through a couple of menus and selected a galactic map.

"Her approval rating is not high because she's cute and adorable. It's because eighty-nine percent of the galaxy's citizens are morons. She has yet to take the throne, and she's already the most popular ruler in recent history. This is a nightmare."

Dake studied the hologram, unsure of how to reply. The display showed a galactic map of approximated approval ratings. Red indicated positive ratings; yellow, negative. Most of the galaxy was red, with tight clusters of yellow around Casifel's home system and several other systems that were informally known as the Galactic Center of Power.

Casifel's long, slender white antennae were swept back and low on the top of his head. Although Casifel rarely displayed this particular expression, Dake recognized it as a sign of agitation and anger.

"Yes," Dake said finally. "A nightmare, indeed. And it's coming on the heels of the term of one of our galaxy's lowest-rated rulers. Every day he becomes more and more despised. Luckily, the galactic approval rating is nothing more than a statistic. High or low, the rating provides a ruler with no more and no less authority to change our regulations or their enforcement."

Casifel's voice was low, nearly a growl. "Regulatory authority has nothing to do with this disaster. It's the insane confluence of her galactic approval rating, her home planet's ridiculous wealth valuation, the idiotic rise in radical altruistic values in the galactic congress, and our inconceivable inability to control this creature."

"Yes, Consul. It is a calamitous alignment of inopportune proceedings. Most unfortunate. However, we did warn you that the impact of the sitting ruler's heavy-handed, despotic approach could result in a swing in the galactic congress sentiment." Dake marveled at how much damage Casifel had done in the relatively short time he'd had control over the galactic leader selection and grooming process. *Ah well*, he thought. *One way or another, Casifel's incompetence will take care of itself.*

Casifel let out a roar, slamming his hands on the data pedestal. "My species does not pay your species planetloads of galactic credits to merely commiserate with our quandaries or to appreciate the obvious. We pay you planetloads of credits to resolve our problems and remove obstacles." Casifel pointed a long, thin white finger at Dake. "We pay you planetloads of credits because your species offers the best blend of technical intelligence and political discretion we can buy. Please tell me you have another strategy to convince this primeval miscreant, this Sally Ann, of the error of her ways."

Dake placed his three-fingered purple hands together in a steeple to calm himself. "I have no additional strategies that can be executed in the short amount of time we have remaining. I am sorry, Consul."

Casifel took a deep breath, then waved a hand at Dake. "I won't accept that. Let's go over our options again. Humor me. First, assassination. Any viable options there?"

"Consul, even if you ignore the absurdity of assassinating the very individual your office is responsible for overseeing, you know very well that your species has spent the last thousand years designing, redesigning, and tweaking the anti-assassination system. Moreover, we have explored every possible option for circumventing it: hacking, the physics breakthroughs, clone swapping, simulated natural disasters. Congratulations are in order for your species' system design, as we have found nothing that will beat it. Any assassination attempt is folly, unless . . ."

"Unless what?" Casifel asked, his antennae rising.

"Unless you personally were to perform the assassination. We have identified—"

Casifel cut him off with a gust of laughter, but Dake was satisfied that the seed was planted.

"That will not happen," Casifel grunted. "What about once again attempting to force Advisor Alspotemis to assist us in evolving Sally Ann's objectives? Perhaps he didn't take us seriously enough last time. What if we threatened his home world or family?"

"We consider Advisor Alspotemis irrevocably turned. He would likely expose any such deceptive maneuvers to the masses. And right now, any such incident could lead to galactic revolt."

"Yes, of course," Casifel said with a sigh. "I was naive to think we could count on even *his* neutrality. Her ability to manipulate is unmatched." He rubbed his neck in frustration.

"I would not consider her effect on Advisor Alspotemis manipulation—at least not in the way you or I think of manipulation. Simply stated, after a two-year onslaught of physical affection and genuine innocent love, Advisor Alspotemis has been completely and totally *won over*. And before you ask, we have the same opinion of Professor Catibina, her educational overseer. They have become sympathetic to Sally Ann's ideologies."

"Innocent love?" Casifel repeated. "This child, this *monster*, is hardly innocent. I find it inconceivable that *you* have been unable to influence her in two years. Our model has worked for thousands of years, across thousands of species and races. Yet somehow, she can indoctrinate the very agents who are paid to condition her."

"Well, your methods might have been more success-ful—if *you* had made different choices concerning her advisors early on. Different advisors that would have been a little less indulgent and a little more . . . ruthless, shall I say? And even then, Sally Ann is stubborn. She seems to have an unshakable will. Unfortunately, we knew so little about humans—especially young females such as Sally Ann. It is a pity."

"Cat! You're here!"

Despite wearing her fine blue dress and a rather uncom-fortable pair of dress shoes, Sally Ann broke into a run and closed the distance between herself and Professor Catibina quickly. Sally Ann ran directly into Catibina without slowing, collapsing into a hug.

Catibina returned the hug, wrapping her paws around Sally Ann tightly.

"Spot and I just went on the most wonder-filled walk," Sally Ann exclaimed. "We saw a whole flock of air jellyfish. Spot says they're called gelifawks, but I'm still going to call them air jellyfish. They just float on the wind. We also saw mushrooms taller than my head! And in the lake, we saw something curious. It's like a combination of a frog and a tur-tle. It has a shell, but it hops. It's sort of sad—it can't hop high like a frog because it's heavy, so it just kind of flops. I don't know whether to call it a trog or a frogurtle. Cat, you should have come."

Cat broke the hug first, though Sally Ann held on a moment longer. Then she let go. Cat was continuously amazed, but also secretly delighted, at the girl's need for affection.

"I *couldn't* come," Catibina said with a sigh. "That's because *someone* had to rearrange the schedule for the day." She gave a knowing look. "When you do this, Miss Sally Ann, you know it has a ripple effect. It impacts a great number of people. You need to stay on your schedule. We have little time and much to do."

Sally Ann's face scrunched up. "I'm sorry," she said softly. "But it was such a beautiful morning—I thought I would go mad without a walk. And it would probably be bad for the galaxy to have a mad queen, although I do like the sound of that. And honestly, I'm really getting tired of learning about galactic regulations and protocols."

Cat put her paws on Sally Ann's shoulders, her whiskers twitching. "Miss, I know it's difficult. But it's for the good of the galaxy. The galaxy needs you."

Sally Ann pushed Cat's paws off of her shoulders and glared. "It's you people who are mad! I didn't choose to be queen. I just want to go home." Her lower lip quivered, but she fought it off. "And if I can't go home, then you must push me on the swing!"

Consul Casifel angrily waved the galactic map off the data pedestal, pivoted, then began to pace. Dake smirked to himself, recognizing this as a further sign of tension. Well-deserved tension, of course—after all, Casifel's species had managed the selection, procurement, grooming, and handling of the empire's leaders for well over a thousand years. His species managed the galactic kings and queens and selected their advisors and teachers. His species had influenced the structure that had led to over a thousand years of relative peace. They had ensured that terms were short, and the rulers were unknowns.

This influence, in short, allowed his people to rule behind the scenes while appearing to simply manage the process—a scenario that had provided fantastic wealth and prosperity for his planet and other friendly trading partners while great sections of the galaxy lay in horrific poverty.

Casifel had come to power shortly before the last selection. He had been randomly handed a perfectly malleable, willing king. So what if he was a brutish, racist old fool? Casifel had pushed the orange crustacean to further galactic oppression in order to give himself—as well as his people—more power and more profit. Everything had gone perfectly.

Until Sally Ann.

"Dake, you seem to have given up," Casifel said, attempting to sound calm. "You seem to lack the motivation required. Do I have to remind you that your species has lived a comfortable existence largely due to our species' relationship? If we fall, you fall. Do you believe that there will be no personal consequences for your failure?"

"My failure? I don't understand. Forgive me, Consul, but it was your recommendation to assign her particular advisor and educational overseer due to their resemblance to the human companion species they call dogs and cats."

Casifel sighed, clearly losing what little patience he'd managed to gather. "Yes—after *you* informed me that their species had the highest chance to calm the child. She was so inconsolable at first. No one could stand to be around all that pitiful sobbing. It was untenable." Casifel smacked his hand against the data pedestal and shouted an expletive, then continued to pace.

"I merely answered your direct question about effective ways of soothing the child," Dake said, placing his hands together. "I never recommended Alspotemis as a personal advisor. Just as I never recommended Professor Catibina as her educational overseer. Neither has the right disposition for furthering your political objectives. This is all well documented."

Dake paused, smiling slightly when Casifel's back was turned, then continued his lecture.

"The girl has demonstrated an astonishing degree of understanding of galactic protocols, regulations, and legislation. I would venture to say a dangerous amount. She has the political skill and the support to achieve dramatic change. This is a grave situation for you and your home world."

Casifel stopped pacing. He flew at Dake, stopping only when his face was millimeters from his operative's—significantly past the customary amount of personal space, even for Casifel's species. Dake was pleased with the level of agitation he was achieving with the consul and now had to work hard not to show physical signs of his delight.

"Well, try again! I will not let you paint me as solely responsible for this catastrophe, you worm. If my neck is on the line, so is yours." Casifel stepped back slightly and glared at Dake for a few moments before finally turning away. He returned to his rant as if the encounter hadn't happened, but his antennae remained flattened against his head. "The little devil seemed so weak, so pathetic. I was certain we would be able to assert a level of control over her like we have never achieved before. I wanted an educator who could develop her political dexterity beyond all others. I wanted a puppet leader who could fine-tune our control. Now we have created a monster. *Try again!*"

"I have already sent another request to Professor Catibina, despite the probability of any progress being infinitesimal. But again, I do not understand your use of the word *we*." Dake repressed another smirk and moved slightly to make eye contact with Casifel. "Your requests and decisions are well chronicled. I even submitted to you several heterodoxy protocol entries expressing my concern with your decisions, all of which went unanswered."

Casifel waved off Dake's words once again. "You know I have no time or interest in lower-level protocol entries. You had no reason to imagine I would review those. I will not let you evade your responsibility here. You are still under my employment."

Casifel paused then, thinking. Judging by his perking antennae, Dake presumed some idea had occurred to the consul.

"What about threatening her home planet?" he asked. "Wouldn't that gain her attention?"

"You know as well as I do that her home planet is untouchable. As the newest planet in the empire and the home of the future queen, Earth is simply under too much scrutiny. And it is under full protection by the Centerians, who are infatuated with human culture, music, and art—as is most of the galaxy. Humans' ability to love to the point of tragedy is so compelling that their art and music is some of the most highly sought in the universe."

"I've heard their music and seen their art. It's crude, raw, and clumsy. Half of it is obscene. It is a short-lived fad that will soon evaporate along with their newfound alliances. It's only a matter of time."

Dake watched as Casifel stretched his head left and right and exhaled—the consul's anger was dissipating. Dake had to keep twisting the knife. "Yes, but it's time we do not have. Once Sally Ann is installed, she will move quickly."

"I know. We can't touch her, we can't trust her aids, and we can't destroy her home planet. So we must mute her power. We must change galactic sentiment. Why do they like her?

How can we sabotage her? How can we tie her to Earth's history of violence?"

"The issue is Sally Ann herself. She is the perceived embodiment of Earth. She is viewed as innocent, delicate, and utterly nonthreatening. Regardless of who she might become, she is not now perceived as a symbol of warfare, especially when she is compared to your orange crustacean, who is currently oppressing the galaxy. She is a breath of fresh air compared to that tyrannical lobster."

Casifel's smile disappeared as quickly as his antennae returned to their swept-back position. "He is maximizing galactic profits!" Casifel insisted. "He has advanced our holdings and increased our wealth. And yes, he is universally hated, but that is the beauty of this structure: *he* is hated, not us." Casifel shook his head, returning to the subject at hand. "Well, focus on Earth's people, then. Leak images of battles, conflict, and death. Earth has been so careless with their content. It will be simple."

Dake again smiled, projecting as much condescension as possible. "We have, of course, studied this option as well. While Earth has been barbaric and cruel, their weapons and defenses are ancient. Any images of war will not invoke fear, just pity and melancholy. And those intelligent enough to predict the result of Earth's violent passions combining with our advanced technology likely desire a change in galactic power anyway."

Consul Casifel looked up and howled. Dake was pleased.

It had been easier than he'd expected. Casifel was a clumsy exploiter who needed to be taken care of. Besides, Dake's species had been in the background for too long. It was time for a change. Change and chaos created such interesting opportunities.

Catibina pushed Sally Ann forward just as the child's momentum had slowed to a near stop. Sally Ann's blond curls flew chaotically in the wind. Catibina was unable to stop a purr from rising deep in her throat. Sally Ann had long ago perfected the ability to pump her legs and maintain a vigorous pendulum motion on her own. But both she and Catibina found some curious comfort in this swinging ritual.

"Cat?" Sally Ann asked quietly. "How will people treat me when I am queen?"

Catibina pushed again. It was all rhythm and timing. Even before Sally Ann had voiced this question, Cat had realized she would have a hard time hurrying Sally Ann to her next appointment—what with the sun shining and the pleasant buzz of passing gelifawks above. But this question seemed more important to Sally Ann than most of her other inquiries, so Catibina allowed herself a few moments to chat with her protégé. It was a welcome respite now that she had that absurd request from Dake to address.

"I suppose they will treat you with wonder and adoration, at least at the start. But how people treat you over time depends on *you.*"

Sally Ann pushed her legs out, nearly touching one of the passing gelifawks that floated by with the toe of her left shoe.

"Good. Because I don't want to be treated with wonder and adoration. I just want to be normal."

"Well, Miss Sally Ann, that may not be entirely realistic. Your species is still somewhat isolated. Most people in the galaxy only know Earth from its art and music. To many, you will always be something different, something mythical. But you will find friends who discover you are the same wonderfully ordinary Sally Ann you always have been. Those are the people you need to hang on to."

"People like you and Spot."

"Yes, people like us." She cleared her throat. "Now, let's change the subject. We talk all the time about *how* to change galactic laws, regulations, and protocols, but we rarely discuss *what* to change. Have your priorities changed?"

"We've been over this," Sally Ann said with a dramatic sigh. "My priorities have not changed."

"It's my job to make sure your objectives are clear. Please answer my questions, Miss. It's important." She continued to lightly push Sally Ann each time she swung back.

Sally Ann paused, performing three or four more swings before beginning her answer.

"First, we must use more of the galactic taxes to feed the starving systems in the eastern spiral arms. I've done the math. We have the capabilities and resources for all to be fed. There's no reason for anyone in the galaxy to suffer. And we must stop slavery. It's far too rampant here."

"Miss, you know there is no slavery." Cat said it quickly, surprised at her own defensive tone.

"Call it whatever you like," Sally Ann said, unable to help herself from huffing slightly in irritation. "Permanent servitude is still basically slavery. Everyone knows it. They just won't admit it. It must stop. Every species, race, and individual must have the freedom and opportunity to advance to full potential. Entire planets are being stifled, held back through unfair tariffs and trade restrictions. There must be freedom throughout the galaxy. And there *can* be. Also, my galactic government should have the least power and influence possible. The galaxy and its societies must be allowed to trade, grow, and prosper without galactic government interference." She paused, then nodded. "Those are my objectives, Cat."

Catibina chose her words carefully. "Miss, it's wonderful that you have such lofty principles and values. But surely you understand that these objectives will be received negatively by many in power. You will need to compromise. You will need to move slowly."

"No!" Sally Ann shouted. She leaped from the swing just at the peak of its forward arc and athletically twisted in midair, facing Catibina as she landed.

Catibina took a surprised step back and watched Sally Ann catch and steady the swing. Catibina admired the way the girl was rapidly changing from a small adolescent to a young human woman.

"No. It's one thing to be Alice. But if I must be the Red Queen, I will not compromise."

Catibina recognized the reference—she had read much of Earth's literature—and felt a pang of guilt.

"I've been taken from my home planet, my friends, and my parents," Sally Ann continued. "My childhood has been stolen. My *life* has been stolen. I won't let that sacrifice go to waste. I won't meekly follow orders. You and my many other advisors, teachers, and doctors have boosted my aptitude in thousands of areas. You've improved my memory and my intelligence. I clearly understand my power and my position. And I understand the level of support behind me in the general populace and in the senate. I know every law, regulation, and protocol. And so I *will* end slavery. I *will* end hunger. No one can stop this."

A lone cloud drifted in front of the sun, momentarily muting its glow. The gelifawks fell silent.

"I believe you, Miss. But this is a galaxy, not a planet. The changes you propose are massive, with great ripples. No one can predict the outcomes. And queen of the galaxy or not, once the changes have begun, you cannot control them."

Catibina paused, but Sally Ann remained silent.

"Once, there was galactic war, with death and destruction everywhere. Today, there is stability. The central government may have brought inequity and even some suffering, but its policies have also established equilibrium. The wars are over. Despite all our capabilities, we cannot foresee the consequences of your proposed changes. You must understand that change is a dangerous thing."

Sally Ann stepped forward. She looked up, met Catibina's yellow-gold eyes, and smiled pleasantly. "Everyone tells me I was selected by random chance. Well, I don't believe the universe works that way. I must have fallen down this rabbit hole for a reason." Her smile ran away from her face. "This galaxy has the resources and the technology to be in true harmony. The only thing preventing it is fear of change."

The lone cloud moved on, and the bright sunshine returned. The gelifawks restarted their buzzing right on cue.

Professor Catibina gave Sally Ann a wide, toothy Cheshire grin. It was not a natural expression for her species, but she knew Sally Ann would appreciate it.

"Well, Miss Sally Ann," she said, "if anyone can change the galaxy, it's you."

Despite there being over one hundred billion planets in the Galactic Empire, only one hundred thousand honored guests could attend the coronation live. Of course, many species couldn't withstand the Earthlike conditions anyway. But largely, the limitations were due to logistics and security. The planet had been chosen not only for its compatibility with Sally Ann's physical needs but also for the majestic thousand-foot waterfall that would serve as the backdrop for the coronation.

The air around the enormous silver stage glimmered from the protection of a force-field security dome. Great silver banners displaying the Galactic Empire symbols decorated each side of the stage. Two polished silver Galactic Defense Guard landing ships flanked the banners.

Of the one hundred thousand honored guests, less than a hundred were inside the security bubble, and at least one-third of those were Galactic Defense guardsmen. One of the hundred honored guests inside the bubble was, of course, Consul Casifel himself.

After all, the coronation was in many ways his show.

Consul Casifel stood stoically. He was dressed in his Galactic Empire uniform, black with silver trim. His ceremonial sword rested on his hip.

He knew that many of the anti-assassination protections were built around repelling a large attack force. And once the coronation got underway, the security dome would be impenetrable. Any massive assault would fail, and any covert operation would be dead upon arrival.

Unless, of course, someone had an agent inside, already inside the dome. To prevent this, the artificial intelligence anti-assassination program interviewed and reviewed everyone inside the dome. It could detect any interviewee's evil intent or covert plot.

As overseer of both the coronation and the anti-assassination program, Casifel had ensured that everyone was interviewed. Everyone but himself.

"She looks beautiful, doesn't she?" asked Professor Catibina, gesturing toward the figure on the stage.

"Yes," Alspotemis replied. "Though I am surprised by her attire. I would have guessed she would have stayed with her simple blue dress. I have never seen her choose red before or anything so garish. Do you know what the symbols mean?"

She nodded. "Apparently, they are ancient symbols commonly used on playing cards in her culture. It's an homage to a fictional story she is quite taken with. I think the masses will like this new look. She also seems to carry that heavy scepter with ease. I'm glad we didn't skimp on her physical training."

Most of the ceremony was over. Alspotemis and Professor Catibina were seated in the front row. On the stage, Consul Casifel and Pricampria, the reigning galactic diva and tonight's coronation emcee, were stationed to the left of the silver throne. Sally Ann was to the right.

Diva Pricampria had performed a stunningly tragic rendition of "Galactic Lament," as well as a more upbeat Earth song, "We Are the Champions," by the band Queen, now an intergalactic hit. All that was left now was the crowning of the queen and her coronation speech.

As Diva Pricampria asked all to rise, a hush fell over the crowd. She and Consul Casifel walked in front of Sally Ann. The diva held a jewel-encrusted silver tiara on a silver pillow.

"Lady Sally Ann," said Casifel, "as is tradition, we are honored to coronate you in the custom of your home world. After I touch this sword to your shoulders and head, I will place the tiara upon your head, and then you will be the galactic empress. May you reign with grace and beauty." He smiled widely, baring his large teeth. "Please kneel."

Sally Ann smiled back and knelt before the consul, the diva, and the beings representing over one hundred billion planets, who were all watching intently. She bowed her head.

Casifel suddenly felt nervous. He knew he would have only an instant. His hope was that the armed nanobots circling the proceedings would be confused. The consul knew the bots had no protocol in response to a successful assassination; that bit of programming was considered unnecessary. Once the deed was done, they would become inert. He also knew that if he didn't try, he would eventually be killed by his own people for his incompetence anyway.

Casifel drew the ceremonial sword—which had been secretly sharpened to a razor edge. He touched it against one of Sally Ann's shoulders, then the other. Next, in a move he had practiced several hundred times, he swiftly pulled the sword upward. Gritting his teeth and closing his eyes, he swung it with all the force he could muster at Sally Ann's neck.

The sword carved the air and then abruptly stopped with a clank. Sharp pain from the impact transferred from his hands to his arms, then seemed to explode in his sensitive antennae.

He opened his eyes, expecting to see the sword sliced deep into Sally Ann's neck. Instead, he saw Sally Ann staring up at him. She was crouched low, holding her silver scepter with both hands over her head, his sword tight against it.

In one smooth motion, she twisted the sword away, spun around for momentum, and swung the heavy scepter into Casifel's neck, breaking it.

The crowd exploded in screams, gasps, and other expressions of surprise and horror. The nanobots dove in quickly but took less than a second to determine that Casifel was no longer a threat. A squad of silver Galactic Defense guardsmen stormed onto the stage between Sally Ann and the audience, scanning for additional threats. With trembling hands still holding the pillow with the tiara, Diva Pricampria stood in shock, watching it all. Eyes wide, she swayed slightly.

Alspotemis and Catibina exchanged glances, preparing themselves to rush to Sally Ann's side to comfort her. But they both held back after glimpsing her steely, determined eyes.

Stepping over Casifel's body, Sally Ann put one hand on Diva Pricampria's shoulder, steadying her. She whispered into the diva's ear. Sally Ann then took the tiara from the silver pillow and placed it on her own head.

She took several steps forward, parting the squad of Galactic Defense guardsmen. The crowd fell into silence as their new queen addressed them.

Sally Ann gathered herself, adrenaline from the encounter giving her strength. "Beings of over one hundred billion worlds, of all species and all races: greetings. I address you as queen of the galaxy. I did not choose this title or its duties. I've been told it was random chance, like falling down a rabbit hole."

Sally Ann looked over at Catibina, meeting her eyes with a small smile. "At first, I was afraid, but then I came to understand that this is all an adventure. And I've learned that very few things are impossible. I've learned to believe that cats and dogs can talk, that jellyfish can float on the wind, and that I can slay the Jabberwock."

She gestured at Casifel's body and looked at the confused crowd. She decided to continue instead of explaining herself.

"For the next five years, I have great power and great responsibility. I have been learning about a galactic empire I did not even know existed before my selection. But here is what I have learned: There are enough resources, technology, and capabilities for all planets and all creatures to thrive. There is no reason for poverty, hunger, or suffering."

Sally Ann listened for a moment to the crowd's cheers. Then she stopped them by raising an open palm.

"We will end financial servitude. We will end poverty. We will end hunger. We will end suffering. We will share our resources, our technology, and our capabilities across the galaxy." Her face grew darker suddenly, as if a shadow were passing over her face. "No planets will be allowed to live in extreme luxury. But if they contribute, they will still be able to thrive and prosper. I understand this is a great change. Some will resist. But I can assure you I will use the might of the Galactic Defense Guard, my planet's new allies, and all my will to help these planets understand their new reality."

With that, the Red Queen turned around and picked up Casifel's silver sword, holding it up to the crowd.

"And if they can't understand their new reality, then . . . off with their heads!"

The End

ACKNOWLEDGMENTS

A short story collection is a different animal than a novel, so I went through another big learning curve with this project. Luckily, I had much help and support. I would like to start with my wife, Melinda. Once again, she responded to my constant, impatient requests to read my stories and listen to my insecurities with nothing but grace and positivity.

I want to thank my beta readers—Josh, Mary Alice, Rob, and Louise—for their feedback. I would also like to thank my family, friends, and everyone who supported my first novel. Their compliments and encouragement gave me the mental energy to continue my writing.

My publisher, Lily Coyle with Beaver's Pond Press, provided sound advice and guidance. Kellie M. Hultgren did a fine developmental edit. I can't thank Ruthie Nelson and Angela Wiechmann enough for a heroic copy edit that vastly improved these stories. Thanks to Taylor Blumer for wrapping up the editing process with the proofread. If you love the book cover and interior design as much as I do, please join me in thanking the very talented Athena Currier.

Here's a deal: if you keep reading, I'll keep writing,

Kevin A. Kuhn, October 31ˢᵗ, 2019

PS: If you enjoyed these stories, consider checking out my full-length novel, *Do You Realize?* It won the 2018 eLit Gold Medal for Science Fiction and was a finalist for four other literary awards. It also spent time as a number one bestseller on Amazon in four countries. You can find it on Amazon, Kindle, Audible, Kobo, Nook, and iTunes, and it's available for order at most booksellers.